Famous Liberian Folklore

D. OTHNIEL FORTE

DEDICATION

This book is dedicated to all the children of Liberia, especially those that lost their lives during the senseless civil crisis. For those that live, here is a piece of timeless Liberian folklore

For a Liberian in many ways …. Peter Pinney.

To our next generation; Baby Meshach, McAngel, Marley, Lucas, Reuben, Othniela, Roosevelt (Roro), Achilles (the fox), Achilla (Ma Annie),

This book is also for these special ones, you are special and loved; Abednego, Mark, Josh, Breanna, 'Mother' Grace, Abralyn, Fouad, Amal, Cianneh and Damian, Uche, Edwin (Sure-sure) and Herman, Destiny and Eden, Tricia and Richie, Vanessa, Joslyn, Josh, Racheal, Eslee (Doctor), Ommi, Ebony, Mbochi (Emily), Ezinne (Sarah), Ugochukwu (Nathan), Ethan and Justice, Daniel, Praise-Salome, Daneesha, Ebory and Fabian, Sankara, Rachel- Danielle, Janiel, Kweku, Nana Adjewa, Paa Kwesi, Sheldon, Queen and Babygirl, Musu, Tara.

CONTENTS

ACKNOWLEDGMENTS

The stories in this book come from all over Liberia. They are not limited to any one tribe. They are in fact the story of the people of Liberia. The real credit goes to the great Story Tellers who sit around fire hearths, under the full moon and keep the children glued to their every word as they keep the Oral Tradition of this nation alive. Although most of these great minds are gone, their memories live on in the hearts and minds of all who have had the honor to hear them tell of the valor of our ancestors.

The attempt to retell traditional myths is not new, many have done so before but special credit goes to the Liberian Society of Authors, for publishing versions of these stories for the International Book Year, 1972. This major step boosted Liberian folklore and we must note said, for it greatly influenced the author in his quest as a modern Liberian folklorist seeking to highlight Liberian literature. I am indebted forever to the authors that contributed to that mammoth effort. This book would not have taken its proper form without their work.

Lastly, I must credit our traditional leaders, elders, teachers, storytellers, Paramount Chiefs, Clan Chiefs, town chiefs, Christian missionaries and other religious leaders who dedicated their lives and services to keeping our oral tradition alive. We say thank you.

I cannot close without noting the special love, care and support of my family from whom I stole time to make this project a reality. Mother Dear, Harri, my love, my brothers, Macho, Eman, Abel, and Rebazar, Musu, Evelyn, Reuben II, Othreniel, McAlvin, Jewel.

Chapter 1

Our Brother's Choice

Near the Lake Piso, there lived three brothers. They were hunters. The eldest was Momolu, next was Varfey and Boima was the youngest. One morning, they decided to go deeper into the mystical forest. They wanted a challenge and the ordinary games were no longer fun to them. They gathered their gears and left for their adventure.

They ventured so far into the forest that they were beginning to fear they might get lost, so they decided to rest, eat and set up their traps in the area. As they unpacked, they noticed that the huge tree under which they were resting looked different.

"There is just something odd about the place." Momolu said.

"What do you mean?" asked Boima.

"It's hard to explain, but I feel funny," added Varfey.

"Okay, you two are making me scared. Before we do anything else, let's check the place," said Boima. Thus, they investigated and soon realize this must have been a shrine long ago, and truly, it was. It was the most popular and powerful shrine of the people who settled the land before them. In the middle of the shrine, they noticed an unbelievable sight. There was one large sac of gold!

Whatever joy they felt was short-lived. "It is the shrine of Sande-Ynana," Varfey whispered fearfully. He squirmed and groaned about. Sande-yana was the women society's Goddess, who was reputed to be dangerous and cruel, when crossed. Every man in the clan knew better than to defile her shrines or offend her priestesses, some even refused to mention the name. They believed that she could make one's wife, sister or daughters barren. On the other hand, she could give them so many children until the person got weary, old and eventually died in childbirth. She was one Goddess no one messed with.

Anyone who wanted to have children or for his sister or female relations to have one, had to appease her. They would normally leave that up to the females in the family who would go to the Priestesses and conduct a special ritual of appeasement. Rarely did a man venture there for fear of saying or doing the wrong thing. It is not hard to see why these brave hunters would tremble when they found themselves in the heart of the feared Goddess' shrine especially with no female around to guide them.

The eldest brother, Momolu, advised, "I think that we should back out and find another place to rest, preferably far from this shrine."

"Yes," whispered Varfey, nodding furiously his agreement, fearing to utter his words loudly. He did not want any misfortune befall him or his future wife.

Then Boima, the youngest stared with eyes wide and full of greed. He said, "This is no longer an active shrine, it had no Priestess guarding it, nor did anyone attend to it." He reasoned. "You two are afraid for nothing. It is not as if we are trespassing or defiling an active shrine. The villagers who tended this shrine had long died and the Goddess' Priestesses had moved on. There was nothing to fear."

His two brothers still did not seem convinced. "I don't like it one bit." One said.

He said, "Look, if this was an active shrine, would we not be dead by now? Would the Goddess not strike us dead already?" This seemed to make sense but the others did not want to take the risk. He reached out and touched the gold.

His brothers crunched, one tried to stop him, "No! Don't do that." However, he was not fast enough.

"Why am I not dead?" he asked. "This is real gold before us. I mean wealth beyond anything we know and you would pass it up based on fear?"

"Prevention is better than cure," said Varfey.

Eventually he managed to impress upon them to take just a small amount of gold. "We take a small amount; nothing large. This is not as if we are stealing or anything. This gold and the shrine have been abandoned long ago. No one is using it."

Varfey refused to have any part in it. "I wish nothing to do with this. You two can do as you wish, but leave me out. I just wanted to leave."

The eldest brother also wanted to leave. "I also want to leave this place, but think of it Varfey. Boima will not leave this issue alone. You know him. What shall we do? We want to go, he wants to take some gold before he goes, so let us leave him to take his gold and face all the troubles alone. In the end, we will leave this place. The sooner he takes it, the sooner we can leave. We all get what we want." He figured that if taking the gold was what was needed to be done to get out of there, he did not mind. Thus, they left with Boima taking a small amount of gold along with him.

They hunted and caught a huge game, but their minds kept going back to the gold of the shrine. They could not understand why their brother was still alive after what he had done. The two brothers decided to send Boima into the nearest village in search of some things and to inform the king that they had caught a leopard. As was the custom, any leopard caught had to be taken to town and presented to the Chief who would perform a special ceremony.

Thus, the little brother went to town with the news. On his way, he kept thinking, "If only I could get rid of my brothers, I could take all the game add it to my gold and live a wealthy man the rest of his life." He began devising ways to achieve that end.

Back in the forest, Momolu told Varfey his younger brother, "Look, our little brother was right, I think. Up to now he is still alive why don't we take the gold for ourselves and return to town as wealthy men?"

"I don't know what is happening, but I want no part of that gold. We have a big leopard. We can keep hunting and selling our meat. That is enough for me. I don't want to mess with Sande-Ynana or her shrine. After all, I wish to marry one day and when I do, I want children. I won't spoil my chances." Thus, Varfey refused.

After a while, Momolu brought up the topic. "What if you help me take the gold? I know you don't want any of it, but just help me."

"How do you suggest we do that? What will you do that? There is no way to take his gold without him knowing. Just remember, this is our little brother here."

"I am not planning to do anything bad to him," lied Momolu, "all you have to do is help me convince him to leave the gold here in the forest, then I can come back for it later."

"If that is all you want, to convince him, I can try doing that but no more." Varfey said.

"Thank you," said Momolu. Deep down, he thought, "Maybe I should just get rid of both of them. It is true that as long as these two live, I can't have all that gold to myself." Thus, he set in motion a plan to get rid of the others and keep all the gold, plus the extra one he would collect from the shrine.

Meanwhile, Boima, got to thinking, "What if my brothers tell on me when we get back to town? I really don't trust them to keep quiet about this gold. They could go and tell the local Priestess and she could come and claim the gold. I must do something about them. Right now, they are acting as if they do not want the gold but when I start enjoying, they will come and bother me for some of the money. They think they are smart, I should take all the risk and they just enjoy. This I will not allow to happen." He resolved that the gold would not leave in the forest now that he had seen it.

He got to the town and delivered his news. He told the chief he had caught a leopard and would be bringing it to town. He failed to mention his brothers for he had finalized his plans to kill them when he got back. He also bought some palm wine which he made sure was the best quality. He knew his brothers liked wine and would take solace in the drink upon sight. He set off for his return journey and reached just before nightfall.

When his eldest brother saw him, he pretended to be happy. He rushed to him and hugged him. Varfey was not sure what was going on but he did not think much about it. He figured that Momolu had forgotten his plans and decided to let Boima have the gold after all. He asked, "Did you deliver the message to the chief?"

"Yes, I did," said Boima. "He was excited and they are planning a huge welcome for us. He said he would send some men to help us take the animal into town and prepare the feast. As a token of appreciation, he sent this," he produced the palm wine.

"Doggit," said Varfey, "the chief means business oh. He sent all this wine just for us?"

"We will kill ourselves with Palm Wine today!" said Momolu. "By the way Boima, here is something to eat. While you were gone, we caught some bush meat and I cooked it. Eat you must be tired. Let me put sticks on the fire and heat it up for you."

Shortly after, Momolu came over to the tree where they were resting and offered Boima some meat smeared in hot pepper and other leaves, "Here you are. Eat it."

"Thank you, Momolu," Boima said. After a few bites, he could not help but utter, "This is very delicious."

"Eat all, it is yours," said Momolu. He turned to Varfey and offered him another piece. "Here Varfey, eat the last one. I am full and we must finish this before we leave for the town."

Varfey took the meat, hurriedly ate it and pulled the jug containing the wine towards him. He opened it and poured out some wine into the small calabash they had. He took huge swallows and let out a satisfying, "Ahhhh!" with each gulp.

"My man, why are you acting abu on the palm wine? Bring it here," Momolu said.

He passed a bowl over to Momolu who took and all in one quaff and uttered, "Oh yes, this is good palm wine oh."

After several minutes and plenty mouths-full of wine passed back and forth between the two, Varfey decided, "I am going to the river to wash my face and then I will come back and challenge this fine palm wine. We are not taking any back with us because there will be more waiting for us."

"Let me come along for a quick swim. I need a bath before I we go to town," said Boima.

Immediately they left, Momolu rushed for the palm wine and drank. He wanted to drink as much as he could before Varfey returned from the creek.

Meanwhile, at the river, Varfey knelt at the edge of the water, dipped his hand in it and splashed it on his face. He looked up and whispered, "My stomach," but Boima could not hear him. He tried again, this time whit all the energy he could muster, "Boima, help me, my stomach is hurting." Again, to no avail, Boima was immersed deep in the water enjoying his bath. Varfey gulped for air, doubled over and dropped into the water with a heavy splash.

Boima came up after a few deep dives. His body was feeling numb as if he had the cramps, but the sharp pain in his belly was the most annoying. He tried to swim his way to shore but could not power his arms enough. He called out, "Varfey! Varfey!" Nothing. He looked towards the shore and there lay Varfey, head dipped in the water. He could not see clearly, but it appeared he was not moving. He tried to get there, but could not. His attempts at screaming caused great pain in his throat. His legs got weaker. His body felt limp. He felt as if the weight of the water was crushing him. His whole body refused to respond to his commands. He felt darkness engulf him as he swirled down into an abyss of darkness. The lights receded quickly, his eyelids began shutting, his mouth was dry and his head was spinning. The last speckle of light fluttered as if in slow motion, then faded away as his body got paralyze he went under and darkness engulfed him.

Momolu, satisfied for the moment with the amount of palm wine he had consumed, sat down under the huge cotton tree. An intense pain emanated from his bowels. He rolled over, trying desperately to grab hold of the tree or some other steady object he could use for support to stand up. His limbs felt as if the weight of five bags of rice were on them. He tried moving them but no luck. His attempts to call out for help were stopped by dryness in his mouth and he kept swallowing his spit. He needed water, if only he could craw over to the water jug, or even the palm wine a few feet away, he could drink. His head felt swollen, so did his internal organs. He felt as if they were burning inside. He fell over and died.

Varfey awoke in a strange place. As he wondered about his surroundings, the most beautiful woman he had ever seen approached him and assisted him on his feet. They walked a few paced and she motioned for him to kneel down. He did and then another female approach them, stood over him and informed him that she was the Shrine Goddess. She explained that, "You are here by no fault of your own. Momolu poisoned the meat and Boima did the same to the palm wine. However, since he was innocent, I would grant you another chance to live."

He was angry and tried to speak but could not. When he finally was able to, he said, "Thank you very much." The beautiful maiden next to him took him aside and seated him on a stole.

Shortly after, Boima appeared. The Goddess said, "You have done an evil thing and must be punished. You took the lives of your own family. Taking any life is bad, but taking one's own blood and flesh is horrible. However, I am granting you the chance at redemption. You can spare one live, any one life, but it can't be yours. Since you took your brothers' lives, you must choose one of them."

He pondered the situation a while. He was furious with Momolu. He was not going to choose him under any condition. He would rather select Varfey, who actually, did not want any part in this. Thus, he said, "I select Varfey, please spare his life. He should not have to suffer for my sake."

"Very well then, Varfey it will be," said Sande-Ynana. "Step aside and await your punishment."

Then came Momolu, he appeared and Sande-Ynana bemoaned him for his wickedness and offered him a chance at redemption. She said, "Because of your greed and selfishness, you caused the lives of your brothers. You will be punished severely for what you did. However, I would give you the chance to spare one of your brother's lives. All he had to do was choose one. That person will get to live again.

He did not even think long, there was no way he would allow Boima to live; after all, he had poisoned the palm wine. If he did live, he would collect the gold and enjoy it. Varfey on the other hand, did not want the gold; also, he was innocent in all this. "Varfey is my choice," he said.

"Very well," said the Sande Goddess.

Turning towards Varfey, she said, "Since both of your brothers selected you, the choice is now yours. Which one do you think deserve life the most?"

Varfey now had the power of life over his brothers. Boima poisoned the wine and Momolu poisoned the meat. What choice do you think Varfey will make?

CHAPTER II

Liars and Thieves

The Chief Thief and the Prince of Liars lived together and neither could agree which possessed the greatest power for causing mischief. Every morning they would start the day practically the same. They argued on whose power was greater and which of them could cause the most damage to others. As was always the case they, they could never agree on who was better than the other.

"I am the best thief in the whole chiefdom," said the Chief Thief. "People fear me."

"Look at this liar here. It is me who people fear in all the land. They panic at the mere mention of my name."

"I didn't know you could lie as well," the liar said sarcastically. "I thought you only stole things. And here you are trying to lie to me of all persons."

This back and forth went on often, so one day, fed up with this routine, they decided to have a competition.

"I am tired with your big mouth," said the thief, "so let's put this issue to rest. All you have is just words, after all how much damage can words do? If I decide to close my ears or ignore you, your words are meaningless. Therefore, you set out to do your best (in other words your worst) and let me do the same. We shall see who is better at causing havoc than the other."

"This is the smartest thing you have said recently Mr. Thief. I fully agree with you. Come next week, we will do just that. I choose the eastern part of the chiefdom. You take the west. I shall show you the power of words." Thus agreed, they left the matter.

On the morning of the day they agreed to begin the competition, the Prince of Thief set out west of their home for a very prosperous far away town. By the evening, he had reached the town. He checked it out and marked all the places he wanted to rob. He waited until it was night, then he cast a spell on the town before he began. He stole every jewelry in town and this was a large town. He carried off shoes, clothes and furniture. He returned for the cattle, chickens and ducks. Next, he took all the totems and valuable items decorating the Chief's Palace. Lastly, he kidnapped the chief's favorite wife. He managed to pull all this off without getting caught.

By morning, the kingdom was in chaos. There was palaver in the town. Ma Mary woke up early to begin chores and noticed there was nothing of value in their kitchen. "Mustapha! Mustaphaaa!!!" She screamed her husband's name.

"What! Woman why are you disturbing this early morning?" he answered sleepily.

"You better get over here." She retorted.

"What happened to the things in the kitchen?"

"Why will you ask me that? Were you not the last one in the kitchen last night? By the way what things are you talking about?" he asked.

"Everything! I mean everything. There is nothing here; no pots, buckets or pans for water, nothing!"

"Look, just find a way to fix your kitchen problems and let me sleep," with this, he rolled over and tried to sleep.

Next door, Ma Kebeh entered her kitchen to start her fire. The hut was as empty as when they had just built it. She ran into the main house and shook her husband violently. "Flomo! Flomo! Wake up Flomo."

"Why will you not let me sleep in peace this morning? You know we will soon leave for the farm why can't I catch small sleep?"

"Sleep? If you want to sleep, then you had better find that your son and have him return my things. I have warned you about Yanqueh. Every time he takes things from here to sell it, you don't say anything. However, today, I think you will kill me because when I get hold of him, you and his mother will not recognize him. I will beat him."

"What is it he took again?" he asked.

"He emptied the kitchen."

Flomo was tired. Things were fine when he had two wives, but his home felt like a war zone after adding two more. His third and fourth wives could not see eye-to-eye. They fussed over everything and now that children were involved, they had ample reasons to quarrel. "Garmai, go to Ma Lorpu and tell her to come with Yanqueh." He instructed his older daughter.

"None of my children are going over to that woman's hut. If you want to see her, you should send your other children."

He was not in the mood for all this drama today. "Gorpu, go and tell Ma Lorpu that I want to see her. Oh and tell her to bring Yanqueh."

Similar scenarios went about the town. Angry women woke their husbands who were angrier at being woken up that early than at the news of missing pots or water pails. As they checked their homes, they noticed all their valuables were missing. It was not long when folks began accusing each other of stealing. Old enemies who needed little or no prodding took this out on each other. The situation forced the men of the town into action. Husbands seized spears and rushed through the town seeking culprits and shouting excitedly.

Some ran to the house of the chief's compound, "Chief! Chief, there is trouble in town!" one man shouted. However, they were shocked at the news they received.

The chief sat on the Royal Stool in a pensive mood. His household seemed in disarray. Those attending to him were on edge. "What happened?" asked an elder?

"Ma Korto is missing," whispered the attendant closest to the elder. This was the chief's favorite wife.

"What! What do you mean she is missing? A whole human being can't just vanish like that." The elder seemed worried.

"This morning," continued the attendant, "the chief woke up early and called on Ma Korto to bring him his pipe to start his day. When she did not appear, he got furious and went to check on her only to find an empty bed. We have searched all over the compound but to no avail, she is gone." The chief was in this enraged state when his subjects met him.

The chief was thinking, "Someone had to pay and pay dearly for this. I swear but whom, I don't know. I suspect my in-laws for this. They had taken my wife. I am sure of this. They had come for her at night. Whatever the case, this was trouble."

He ordered his guards to search the town again. This time, they came back with some items, which he inspected. Amongst them was a sword, he recognized as belonging to his brother in law, the chief of the other town. He called his army and they marched to the town and attacked it, the battle cost many lives.

Whilst this was going on, the Thief and the Liar were watching from afar. The Thief was rolling over with laughter as they observed the village in disarray and the people were at each other's throat. The Thief laughed and laughed, but the Liar just smile as they made their way home.

"I told you I am the best." He kept bragging to his friend. "I dare you to better me at this feat."

"Is that all you can do?" interrupted the Liar.

"What do you mean?" the Thief snapped.

"Can you only cause confusion and small war?" the Liar asked. "Now, let me show you what the Prince of Liars can do!"

Mr. Liar went east of their house to a place where two great towns lay close together. The rulers were two powerful chiefs called Saa and Nyuma. In one of these towns, he befriended the wife of Chief Saa. This woman often quarreled with her husband, who was cruel to her.

"Hello my daughter," Mr. Liar greeted her.

"Hello Papay, how are you?" she replied.

"I am fine oh. Please give me water to drink. I am too thirsty." He said in a fake frail voice.

"Sit down Oldman, where are you coming from?" she asked whilst giving him a calabash of cold creek water.

"I am from the west" but she cut him off again.

"Just cool your thirst and rest small. I will I fix something for you to eat."

"Thank you Ma." was all he could manage before she fired another question.

"What brought you to our town? Aren't you too old to be traveling this far all by yourself?"

"I am a Diviner. I am just passing through. The Chief of the other kingdom requested my service." He confided in her.

"So you mean you have powerful medicine?" she inquired. She had heard about the diviners of the East. They were highly sought after. They were reliable and fair.

He ate his food and prepared to leave. He said, "You have been nice to me so let me do something in return for you. Name one problem you wish I me to help you with."

She was in shock. "Do you really mean that? Okay, I have one big problem. My husband is a very difficult man. He sometimes is not as nice to me as he is to his other wives. Maybe it is because I am not from his tribe. Is there anything you can do for me?"

"I might be able to help you, but you must promise me not to tell anyone else." He told her.

"I swear, I won't say a word to anyone else." She said part hopeful and part desperate.

"Okay then," he said. "I will cause your husband to respect you and he will agree with anything you suggest."

"I am so delighted to hear this. I have wanted this more than anything else." She whispered.

"I know a certain medicine," said Mr. Liar, "which will make your husband love you as he has never loved anyone before. But to make this medicine I must have some hair cut from his belly, head and armpits while he sleeps."

"That is no problem, I can get those." She said.

"However, you must use a special knife," With his right hand, he pulled out a horrible looking knife and gave it to her. "Remember, you must use this knife alone or the medicine would not work."

She nodded happily saying, "Thank you so much Oldman. You have lifted my greatest burden. I don't know how to thank you." She watched him leave.

Mr. Liar walked until he was sure the woman could not see him any longer, and then he detoured and went back to the Chief's Court and requested an audience with the chief, the woman's husband.

"Great Chief, I greet you and your elders with peace. I am a Diviner from the lands beyond the mountains. I am on my way to the next kingdom where they asked me to perform Sassywood and other cleansing rituals. However, I had to pass through your great town to warn you of something. The Great Spirits revealed that a terrible thing would befall you soon. Because news of your greatness and kindness has spread, I feel obliged to render this service to you. However, great chief you must act quickly or there would be no way to stop this evil deed from happening to you.

The chief was concerned; he knew that some of the most knowledgeable and powerful Diviners came from that land, so this was not an issue to take lightly. "Everyone leave the court except the most senior elders and Zoes," he barked. People scrambled out of the hall.

"Yes sir." His chief attendant replied.

Alone with his closest confidents, they discussed a bit then finally he asked "What shall I do master Diviner?"

"Yes what shall we do?" another elder asked the Diviner.

A more senior elder interrupted, "Great Diviner, forgive me, but what is the exact nature of the danger our chief is in?"

"Before I can tell you, I must swear each of you to secrecy with the punishment of death for any violator." Do you understand and agree to this?" the Diviner asked.

"We do," they responded.

"The Great Ancestral Spirits revealed to me that the chief's wife is planning to kill him tonight."

"What?" said the chief in disbelief.

They were all shocked and silent. Finally, one said, "If this is the case, then chief to you have to take care, and watch her closely. Master Diviner, how do we catch her? How do we find proof of this plot?"

"This is what you must do chief. Your wife has a special dagger with her. Its handle is carved of fine wood and ivory. At this stage of her plan, the Juju man has performed all the rituals already. It is only left with this one but for her to complete the ritual; she must remove some hair from your stomach and armpit, mix them with some portion and rub it on you using the knife. Once she does this, you are doomed, because, any part of your body she touches with the dagger afterwards, will get rotten and die. You can't allow her to complete the ritual because this magic is very powerful and almost unstoppable. For you to stop it you must catch the person in the act, otherwise, there is no remedy."

Chief Saa was so surprised he could not help but speak out, "This is unbelievable. What more can I do for this woman?"

However, some of the elders were not. Those that had grudge from past with the wife's family pushed him on. "Chief, we must set a trap for her and allow her to continue the ritual. You heard the Diviner; this is the only way to stop her."

The problem was Chief Saa's wife was the favorite sister of Chief Nyuma, who ruled the neighboring chiefdom. The chiefdoms had fought a bitter battle that cost them both. However, as a truce each had married into the family of the other to ensure some peace. This news was certainly not welcome.

"As the Chief, I'm concern about this for one main reason. I fear for my sister's life. If I have no proof of this, we were going to start a war. We need to be careful."

"What careful again?" said one elder. "These people sent this woman here to kill our chief; we can't allow them to get away with it."

"Whatever the case, at least let us make sure we have proof before we act on anything. At least this much I insist we do," said Chief Saa because he still wanted to defer a war.

After careful deliberation, the elders pushing for war won. The leader closed by saying, "We must set a trap and allow the plan to go through to catch her in the act before we act."

With this settled the Chief Liar took his leave and secretly went on to the next town. He requested an audience with the chief and his trusted elders. When the chief granted his request, he swore those present to secrecy upon death for violators. Then he said, "Chief Nyuma, your sister who is married to Chief Saa is in grave danger. The Oracles have shown me a vision. Chief Saa intends to kill her tonight."

This was unwelcome news. The great chief was cautious about going to war with his in-laws. He remembered all too well how, as a child, his father and the elders had talked about the war and its damaging effect. He had received his wife and lost a sister as part of the settlement.

They deliberated on this for a while. Then the chief said, "I do not wish a war nor do I wish to lose my sister completely. If I am not careful, I will end up having the exact things I do not want. Therefore, I will secretly send some guards into Chief Saa's chiefdom. They will disguise themselves as traders and strangers but nearby in the forest our greatest warriors will stand by in case we need them to rescue my sisters."

Hence, they carried out the plan. The warriors were to stay inconspicuous. Some would visit as guests of the King, thus allowing them to be close by when needed.

As was customary amongst the tribes, strangers or merchants passing through paid the chief a courtesy call and if they had to be hosted, the chief would give them one of the houses in his compound for the duration of their transit. As a rule, they treated the guests as royalty.

Thus, Chief Nyuma had some of his bravest warriors disguise themselves as travelers from distant parts. This ruse placed them close enough to rescue the chief's sister.

Chief Saa was even crueler to his wife that evening. He made her do more work and cook for his new guests. He overtly worked her. At night, knowing that she would be very tired, he hoped she would just fall asleep and save him from going to war. If she did nothing tonight, he could convince those war hungry elders that this was just as scare and things would go back to normal.

At night, Chief Saa and his wife went into their hut and lay on their bed to sleep. Truly, the wife was exhausted. She did not want this one chance to pass her by. She hoped that her husband would fall asleep early because if he did not she feared she would doze off to sleep and miss her opportunity at happiness as they lay on the bed she silently prayed he would sleep. He tossed and turned for a while and then he stopped.

Not long after, she heard him snoring. She quickly retrieved the knife and advanced toward the bed. She lifted his cover and removed a string of hair from his belly and then she pulled one from his armpits. She secured these and moved up towards his head intending to cut the hair with the blade. As she touched his hair, he woke up. He had not been asleep. He was only pretending. He grabbed her hand to get a good look at the blade but in the tussle the knife gashed her arm and she screamed. This was all the guards needed as a cue. They rushed into the house to save her.

The palace guards, also on alert, heard the scream and rushed to the scene. As they neared, they saw warriors of the rival village doing the same. A short and bloody fight ensued. The rest of the guards from Chief Nyuma's village that were in the surrounding forests joined the battle and in no time Chief Saa's men rallied in arms. By the end of the week both towns were destroyed and many innocent lives were lost.

It is not good to lie and steal. The consequences can be dire for others, many of who could be innocent. The wickedness of liars and thieves know almost no end. The Chief Liar was as bad as the Chief of Thieves.

CHAPTER III

Tamba and the Ginah

Way back, God visited the earth personally to water it. At times, the water would be too much in some areas so man built bridges to get across. In Lofa, they build a particularly large bridge across the Lofa River. Everything seemed fine and people went about their normal businesses. However, in one of the rocks beneath the bridge, there dwelt a Ginah who was most annoyed with this situation.

The Ginah complained to God often, but on this day, he was just livid. "God," he said, "The constant movement above my head is a bother and something should be done about it."

"You have said your mind, but could you just be patient with humans, they are troublesome but they have some good in them. Can you bear this a little while?" God asked.

"I can't bear it anymore. I am pleading with you God do something about it." The Ginah entreated God. "It is annoying me and unfair.

"What do you wish me to do about this matter?" God asked.

"Maybe you could stop watering the earth or simply get rid of humans." The Ginah said, after all this was his goal.

Of course, God listened patiently, and then He explained, "If I stopped watering the earth plants would die and so would all life forms."

"If that will solve the issue, then I have no problem." The Ginah blurted out. The Ginah did not really mind for it is a spirit being and would not be affect by that, or so he thought.

This went on for a while, eventually God decided to reduce the amount of water used on the earth. This seemed to work for a while, and then Ginah came back complaining.

"Look God, the situation is occurring again, your solution was temporary. Therefore, I suggest that you allow humans and me to sort things out by ourselves.

God did not like the idea. Baffled, he asked. "How can you think that will solve the issue? You are a spirit against human. You have an unfair advantage."

"I swear God it will be fine. Whatever solution we arrive at, man must fully agree otherwise we will not proceed."

God agreed reluctantly but on the condition, "You can't ever use magical powers. If you deal with man, you must do so without any of your powers."

Ginah paused, but he feared that taking too long might make God change his mind, so he greed. He left feeling elated. He was sure this was his chance to get rid of those *disgusting* creatures called man.

Early that morning, when a group of villagers approached the bridge they saw Ginah perking on the stone just off the entrance. He informed them, "There are new rules from now on. The only way anyone of you can cross the bridge is if you submit to a challenge."

"What! You are joking right?" Jummai asked. They were all puzzled and somewhat frightened. It was common knowledge that Ginah hated man, but endured them because God forbade him to harm them.

"In case you are wondering," he further explained, "I have God's approval. All you have to do is freely participate in the test. Otherwise, find another route or return to where you came from."

Now the only other routes available were extremely long and one still had to pass through the dangerous evil forest. This was not an attractive prospect not when the bridge was safer and faster. One person in the group asked Ginah, "What exactly is the test?"

He explained, "I will lie face down and each person wishing to cross the bridge had to lash me a hundred times. Once done, he will in turn give just one lash. While lashing, if I run or don't remain in the same position before a hundred lashes are over, then the person could cross. However, since you humans had many lashes, I will be able to turn over thrice before you end you beating but nothing more. If more, then you are free to pass. If I make it to the end without breaking the rules, then I will give you just one lash."

This seemed good to them. Some figured surely he could not expect to win this challenge. Furthermore, they needed to get to the other side of the bridge and conduct their affairs.

Foolishly, they agreed. Ginah asked them to pick their stick of choice. "Remember, it can be any length or size. You must hit me with the same amount of strength or higher but never with lesser force." He repeated that once a person swings, they could not swing with less energy than the initial swing. You can only swing with the same force, higher strength or harder force. If you fail, I will eat you."

Most of those present that morning agreed to the challenge. Mr. Ginah lay on his stomach and covered his face ready for the blows. One after the other, those that agreed, struck him but midway they failed the test. Those that made it to the end did not survive his one blow.

What they did not know was that Ginah knew man and their ways. He reckoned that many would go for large, heavy pieces of wood. He believed they could not steadily swing a hundred deadly blows. Moreover, if they opted to swing slowly by the end they would be exhausted and unable to hit him with any force that could cause him significant damage. Either way, once a person agrees, the Ginah felt he would have himself a meal.

By the end of the day, the news had spread to all the villages on the other side of the river. Those on the market side were shocked that almost no one from across the water came to sell produce that day. This was highly unusual since this was a major market day that opened once a week. No one could afford to miss this day.

By the next day, few braved the evil forest to get on the other side. Of those that did, even fewer made it through the forest. By the time they reached to the safety of the other side, they learned that many chiefs and family members, concerned about the wellbeing of their loved ones, had gone towards the bridge. They wanted to know what had happened. It was late evening and many had not returned so the villages were worried. When the men broke the news about Mr. Ginah and how he had possessed the bridge it was too late for them to help. It dawned on them that their loved ones had walked right into danger and possibly their deaths. Gloom took over, women wailed and anxiously waited for news, any news.

The situation continued for a while seemingly with no end in sight. The Paramount Chiefs on both sides of the river offered rewards and the hand of their favorite daughters to anyone who would defeat the Ginah and free the bridge. Sadly, none that braved the challenge survived. Others went to seek revenge for their loved ones and did not come back. Soon, the chiefs decided to offer up half of their kingdoms and the right of succession in addition to their favorite daughters. This drew some brave warriors but the end was the same.

Initially, the Ginah believed his plan flawless. It had worked perfectly. After a while, he realized that men were simply avoiding the bridge. Some braved the river and few took the forest route. He had grown accustomed to human meat, but he was simply not getting it. The small he got came far in between. He began roaming into the forest around the edges of the bride on both sides hoping to see a human he could con into accepting his challenge.

Word spread about the land that a Ginah wandered away from the bridge into the nearby forest and towns. People soon ceased to pass that way. They abandoned the villages close to the bridge and ran away.

Pretty soon, the Ginah began roaming afield in search of human flesh. The chief announced that he would give his daughter and half his riches to the man who would defeat the Ginah but few men were brave enough to try. Sadly, those who did, the Ginah killed.

Over in a small village, far from the bridge, lived Tamba. He was a blacksmith who lived with his mother. He was a well-built young man. His arms were huge and he was strong from the toughness of his work. He came to the town intending to sell his wares in the market. Because his village was so far, he made this trip once in two or three months. When he reached the town, he heard the news and was upset. He could not return without selling his goods. This was not an option. He began to think of a way around the problem when he found out that both Paramount Chiefs had offered half their kingdoms and their favorite daughters as reward. He was thrilled. The thought of marrying a chief's daughter was beyond his wildest imagination, not to mention half of a chiefdom.

He decided to take up the challenge. He told no one of this for obvious reasons. He set out to get a few things before his quest. He went into the forest and when he had found what he needed, he headed back to town where he made his intentions known.

"My son, why are you wasting your life?" one asked him. "Don't you have a family maybe a mother, wife or children?" another asked.

"I have an old mother that I look after," he replied.

"Then go back to her and take care of her. Do not try this Ginah, he is dangerous and will only kill you. Do you really wish your mother to lose her son?" a woman asked.

"No Oldma, I do not want my mother to suffer like that." He replied.

"Then just go home," pleaded the woman.

Several older women tried to persuade him, whilst some of the younger people thought he was crazy. When all failed, some of the younger maidens escorted him to the Paramount Chief's Palace. He expressed his desire to kill Mr. Ginah.

After some dialogue, the Chief assured him that if he succeeded, he would be a wealthy young warrior. "I will give you my pretty daughter. She is my most favorite and is still a virgin. I hope you get rid of this nuisance for all our sakes." The chief then gave his blessings and Tamba set out to meet the Ginah.

He boldly approached the bridge carrying his sac on his back and a stick attached to it. Some of his goods were in his hand. Mr. Ginah could hardly believe his luck when he heard and smelt the person approached. He jumped on the bridge to challenge the person. He was shocked at what he saw. There before him stood a Tamba, barely old enough to be a warrior but there all the same. He was food. Meals came so far and few in between that he dared not complain.

"Oh young man, only fools come to this bridge, and I eat fools for supper. Let us not waste time. Lash me a hundred times with your stick or any other wood and I will lash you once," said Mr. Ginah as he stretched his hands.

"Aren't you forgetting something?" asked Tamba.

"Forgetting what?" Ginah asked.

"The part about lying down and covering your face," said Tamba.

"Oh that," Ginah feigned ignorance. The fact was he was in a hurry to eat.

"Yes that," Tamba insisted.

"Ah, very well, I will lie on my stomach and cover my face but see that you beat me well, for one of us must die," Ginah said as he lay on his stomach and covered his face.

Tamba removed from his bag the stick and swung it with a powerful blow. When it landed on the Ginah's skull, he said "One."

Ginah cried out in a loud voice, "Aieeeei!" Tamba swiftly switch sticks as the Ginah quickly turned over, sat on his tail, and held his hands to his head. He moaned and rocked himself back and forth. He looked at Tamba in disbelief. He let out a grunt and said, "Eeeeeyaaaaa!" as he continued to rob his head.

Tamba raised his stick as if impatient then he said, "Are you ready?"

"Who are you, young man?" Ginah asked.

"I am Tamba," Tamba replied.

"Why have you decided to swing this hard knowing you must keep up this amount of strength or more until you finish?" Ginah asked.

Tamba replied, "I know that I can't swing any less but I do not intend to swing any less. In fact, I expect to increase my swings as I go along, take a look at me if you doubt."

"From what village do you come?"

"I come from a distant land where man is brave and strong. Remember that you have turned over once." Tamba said.

"What is it you use to hit me with?" Ginah inquired.

Tamba said, "It is my walking stick and nothing more."

The Ginah looked at him uncertainly, and asked, "Are you sure of that. No one has swung this hard before."

"I am sure. Do you wish to see it?" Tamba offered the stick for inspection.

The Ginah considered Tamba a little and thought, "But he is only a simple young man."

"Here, have a look." Tamba interrupted his thought.

"Okay! Try again; you were lucky. You must have been." Said Ginah as he went back on the floor, braced himself for the blow, and covered his face.

Tamba switch sticks raised it over and above his head and knocked the Ginah's head as he said, "Two!" Just as before, Tamba hurriedly hid the stick behind his back.

Ginah shouted, "Oooohhh! Yayayaya!!!" The Ginah rose to his feet and staggered. He looked at Tamba as if drunk. "I need to enter the forest and get break. In fact, it is unfair. I can't just allow you to beat me up like this. This is too much. I must have a break or we will not continue otherwise!" whined the Ginah.

Tamba said, "You can't! This was your idea. You alone planned this so you must go through. Are you so cowardly and scared of a few blows from a simple young man?"

"Very well, only a few more blows then, I am not scared of you. You are a kid. I have conquered great warriors why would I be scared. This time around, I will not lie on my stomach. I will turn over and lay on my back," said the Ginah.

"Hahahahaha," Tamba laughed so loud.

The Ginah was confused. "What is funny?" He could not figure out what was funny.

Tamba said, "You are funny Mr. Ginah. Ninety-eight more blows, not a few more. Are you this scared or should I tell everyone how worthless you are and can't stand a youth? You will lie down on your stomach with your face towards the ground as before. If you do not want to, I will agree under one condition; that you allow me to start all over and this time I will choose only your eyes or the area just below you navel."

The thought of Tamba striking him below the waste or the eye horrified the Ginah. He reluctantly resumed his position, "But I am not closing his eyes."

"You will close your eyes," Tamba had to remind him. "You set the rules so you must follow them exactly as you planned them." He had no choice but to oblige.

This time, Tamba, raised the stick even higher but just before he could swing the Ginah sneaked a peek and shouted. "Do you have to raise it that high?"

Tamba pretended to be angry and insisted, "Why are you turning around and opening your eyes? You better just close your eyes and forget about how high or low I lift my stick. After all, it is his business and when the time comes, you Mr. Ginah can swing as you wish, but for now, you must close your eyes and await my blows." As soon as the Ginah closed his eyes, Tamba who had raised the stick even higher, let down a crunching blow smashing the Ginah's head with a terrible, crunching crack.

This time the Ginah shrieked in agony. "Aye yayayaya! Oooohhh! Ma-ma-ma-ma. He struggled to his knees; fell over the edge of the bridge into the water and under his rock. He disappeared below it.

Tamba leaned over the railing calling after him. He sang a mocking song:

"Beat a Ginah,
Beat its head
Thrash a Ginah,
Crush its head
Make a Ginah suffer.
Bash its head 'till it's dead,
Then eat it for my supper!"

Below it, the Ginah trembled, and crouched fearfully under its rock. Tamba called but it refused to get out and continue. What it did not know was that when Tamba went into the forest in preparation of the challenge he had made a secret weapon. He hollowed out a termites' hill, put in raw iron ore and charcoal and added glowing coals, pumped in air with leather bellows to make a roaring fire, and smelted iron into a heavy ball. He affixed the iron ball to the end of a long, strong stick, which he used to hit the Ginah.

After it became clear that the Ginah was not going to return, Tamba went to the town and reported that he had passed the Ginah's test. No one believed at first, but upon investigation, the Ginah was nowhere to be found. They asked him to show them how he did that. They stood afar and watched Tamba get closer to the bridge.

Just as he got on the bridge, Ginah shouted out "Who goes there?"

They shuddered in their hiding places but Tamba calmly called out, "It is I, Tamba" and he began singing.

> *I beat the Ginah,*
> *I thrashed the Ginah,*
> *I made the Ginah suffer.*
> *I'll smash his head until it's dead,*
> *And eat him for my supper!*

With that Ginah screamed, "Pass on, Tamba! Move on, be gone, for I seek no trouble from you." That is how he passed over to the other side.

From that day on, anyone who passed the bridge would sing that song when the Ginah asked after him or her. Regardless of which name they called, the Ginah would not come out because he feared that it was Tamba trying to trick him into smashing his head.

He would shout out, "Pass along Tamba; I know it is you playing a trick on me."

Thus, the bridge was free again for all to pass and Tamba received half the kingdom and married the chief's daughter. They had many children and lived happily.

CHAPTER IV

Why Elephant Flees From Goat

Mr. Elephant used to be very greedy. He took advantage of his size too often and all the other animals hated him for that. The only animal that could eat as much was Mr. Spider but the two were not friends and avoided each other.

One day, as was customary during harvest season, the animals went to look for work on the farm. Because of Mr. Elephant's ways, no one wanted to be his partner but Mr. Goat was new in town and did not really mind. Since, he had no friends yet, collaborating with Elephant seemed a good bet. They went out together to find work in the fields.

Fortunately, they got a farmer willing to hire them to do his hoeing, clearing and planting cassava stems.

All the other animals were sorry for Mr. Goat. Some had tried to warn him, others decided to stay out of the issue; after all, it was not their business. The first few days of work, Goat took to his chore with all the determination and energy he could muster. He was thrifty and industrious. He barely noticed Mr. Elephant and the amount of work he did.

Shortly thereafter, Mr. Goat realized that Mr. Elephant was lazy and ate more than he grew. He always opened a nice conversation and did the most trivial work on the farm. He pretended to be exhausted from heavy lifting of tree trunks, which he could easily carry, but chose to take forever just to move one. At almost every stage, when he did manage to take one away, he came back and headed straight for the food and water. This ruse he carried out in variations every day. In the end, Mr. Goat did the brunt of the farm work and had less of the food and water.

He began to tire of this and decided to do something about the situation. He could no longer trust Mr. Elephant with the food or water so he had to find a way around it. On this particular day, he waited for noon when they were both hungry and said: "It is time to eat. Since I am the smallest, I shall prepare the meal whilst you rest," he said.

Mr. Elephant sensing a plot retorted, "Not at all, you are too small and will not make enough. Since it is I who will eat most, because I am larger, I shall prepare your meal and you shall rest."

Mr. Goat thought to himself, "If Mr. Elephant fixes the meal; he would eat as he prepares and my portion will be quite small as usual."

Mr. Elephant on the other hand, had a different fear. He thought, "If Mr. Goat prepared the meal, he would not prepare enough, thus no matter which size he takes, the Goat will get more than him. After all, he reasoned Goat's appetite is less than his." Both tried to outsmart the other and this soon turned into an argument.

The dispute intensified and Mr. Goat shouted, "You are a foolish Elephant. Your big head is all bone that is why you would think like that. Who told you that you could eat more than I could? I can eat more than you so I shall prepare the meal."

The Elephant could hardly believe his ears. It wasn't so much the about insults but what Mr. Goat said. He looked down at Goat, a small and boney animal who barely reached his knee, and protested: "I really cannot believe that you can eat more than I. You are too small. I'm too big I'll always eat much more than you," he let out a load laugh that drew the attention of the other nearby animals.

"Then let us have a competition." Goat suggested.

"Sure, why not." Elephant agreed.

They decided to find as much food as they could haul in readiness for the challenge. They abandoned their faming for the day, and for several hours, they labored to gather a pile of herbs and fruits and grass and roots. This they divided into two equal heaps, and started eating.

Mr. Elephant wasted no time, he ate quickly until his stomach swelled and started to pain him. It was only then that he lay down to sleep a little. He figured he would wait to see how much Mr. Goat would eat.

Mr. Goat on the other hand took his time, he slowly munched, and munched, and when he could eat no more he kept on steadily chewing the same mouthful of grass. This he did until Mr. Elephant fell asleep. Immediately, he removed some of his pile and added it to the Elephant's. The rest he disposed of quietly. When Elephant woke up he saw that Mr. Goat still chewed, but his pile was still large so he fell asleep again. Each time he fell asleep, Mr. Goat moved more of his food to Elephant's pile or elsewhere. For many hours, Mr. Goat chewed on and his pile of food grew smaller and smaller until there was very little left.

Mr. Elephant finally had enough rest and decided it was time to get back to his meal. He was determined to teach this insolent goat a lesson; one he would never forget. When he looked over at Mr. Goat, his heart skipped several beats. "Oh!" He thought. "Am I really seeing clearly, or am I still dazed from my sleep?" Right before Mr. Goat was a very small pile of food and he was still seated in the same position as before and chewing.

Mr. Elephant's pile on the other hand, looked like a mountain. He wondered how Mr. Goat had managed, but he could not dwell too long on that thought, as he had to get rid of his. He feared he might not be able to finish his after all. He was amazed that Goat could eat so much. He could hide his excitement no longer, so he asked, "How is it Mr. Goat that you can eat so much? I am much larger than you, but you have eaten more?"

"Indeed I have," said Mr. Goat. "My appetite is endless. When I am finished this pile of food I shall eat the rest of yours and if I am not satisfied, I swear I'll eat you too!" He said this in such a menacing tone that Elephant became quite alarmed for truly Mr. Goat appeared to have an astonishing capacity.

After some reflections, he rose clumsily to his feet, and said offhandedly, "Brother Goat, I think I'll go into the forest and find some honey. This will increase my appetite." With that, he hurried off into the forest.

In the meantime, the other animals were interested in what the two of them were doing. Some had forsaken their chores to watch, others had taken turns to check on things. None had bothered to tell Mr. Elephant what Mr. Goat had done. They figured it served him right for his greediness and the pain he had caused them. They all knew that Mr. Elephant was lying about the honey, since it did not increase appetite, he was only afraid that Mr. Goat would make good on his threat to eat him.

Thus, it was that Mr. Goat outsmarted and ran Mr. Elephant off. He received the respect and gratitude of all the animals.

CHAPTER V

The Villager Who Dared the Spirits

Near a certain peaceful town, there was a small area of bush land that the town people considered the property of the forest spirits. They would pour libation to the gods of the forest whenever the harvest season approached. This was the tradition of the town and they all respected it, except for one man. He did not care about the beliefs of the townspeople and had little regard for the forest gods or honoring the age-old custom.

He decided one day to start a farm. He told his friend Jomah about this plan.

Jomah was happy for him until he asked, "Where will you be setting it up?" He expected that his friend would choose a spot not far from his own place so that they could be together much the time.

However, that was not what his friend had in mind. He told Jomah, "I intend to establish my farm just outside the town. It will be close to town so I don't have walk far off. However, you know that I will still visit your farm when I can."

This was strange since nobody had a farm so close to the town. Also, the best spots when leaving the town, had been taken by the wealthy elders, and knowing that his friend was not a community leader, Jomah wondered how his friend could get one.

It turned out that his friend had a plan. "I am going to set up my farm on the very bush land that is dedicated to the forest gods. There is no better piece of land in the whole land."

This news alarmed Jomah for this was the last thing anybody in the village would think of doing. He pleaded with his friend. "Why do you wish to bring trouble on yourself? Please try to see reason and not anger the gods in any way. Only bad can come from this idea."

However, his friend told him, "My mind is made up. These old people here are just keeping that perfect spot of farmland; meanwhile they already have the other good land. How do they expect us to get rich? All the other farmlands are far from town, hard to toil alone. If anyone wants to make their harvest increase, they have to hire people to help them clear the land and this requires money. In the end, we just farm to live and nothing more. Well I am tired with this, I will use that land."

Jomah went to his friend's wife and begged her to convince her husband. "Please tell him not to offend the gods. We know that such a thing could only spell trouble for anyone foolish enough to do it. Talk some sense to him."

The wife did her best but failed to discourage her husband. She tried every approach she could think of but he seemed set on doing it, so she let him be hoping his mind would change with time.

As days went by, Jomah tried repeatedly to convince his friend not to carry out his plan, but he only laughed at him every time. He told Jomah that there were no forest gods to offend. He simply did not believe in that tradition or care about the opinion of others. The town's people did all they could to dissuade him, but when they saw it was to no avail, they decided to let him be and to keep their distance for fear of getting into the bad books of the gods.

On the first day, the man went to the bush land and cut some scrub, laying out the area he was going to use for the farm. Afterwards, he went home. The next morning he got up early and began bragging about how he was still alive despite the predictions of the townspeople that he would not survive a day if he annoyed the gods of the forest. He prepared himself and went to the farm.

To his utmost surprise, he found all the other bushes had been cut down. He was certain that he had cleared only a small portion the day before. This made his work much easier and he was glad. He thought to himself, "What if I cut down a tree?"

Therefore, on the second day, he felled a tree and went home. He returned on the third day to discover all the other trees had been cut down, too. "I must be the luckiest man alive," he thought. "I don't have to work hard this year, for some mysterious spirits are my slaves."

On the fourth day when he returned, he discovered that the small fire he had instructed his wife to light the day before, had grown large in the night. It had burnt down the entire farm area leaving it ready for planting. Therefore, he and his wife cleared out one small area. They gathered some unburnt wood and charcoal before going home.

Upon their return on the fifth day, all the unburnt wood and charcoal had been gathered. Thus, they had enough firewood and charcoal, which they took to the village, some to sell and some to use. Before leaving, they put some of the charcoal in a bag and left the rest of the bags on the farm. They also nicely stacked a pile of firewood.

On the sixth day, he went to his farm and saw just what he had expected to see - piles of nicely packed bags of unburnt wood and charcoal. They were arranged one on top of the other and every bag he had brought was fully stacked. "How smart I am," he thought. He was really enjoying this farming thing.

They collected the as much wood and coal and left for home, but on the last trip, he planted one of the grains of rice and instructed his wife to leave few baskets of unplanted rice stalks. During the night, the seeds were planted throughout the field.

He decided that they would not go to the farm on the seventh day. Instead, they would go to the big market in the next town and sell the charcoal and wood they had gotten from the farm the day before. The sale gave them plenty of money more than they had ever had before in their lives.

In the meantime, he bragged more and more each day about how he was still alive and insulted anyone in the village who gave him a hard time about what he was doing. He would ask, "What had happened to your forest gods and what were they waiting for to kill him?" He made a lot of noise, claiming that the forest gods were just a myth and that the people had been deluding themselves all those years.

He continued to behave like this as they waited for harvest time to arrive. The villagers, however, just kept their distance and simply ignored him because they knew that it was only a matter of time before he got what was coming to him.

Eventually, harvest time came and he and his wife went to their farm like everyone else. The man saw that his rice had grown very well and would fetch him more money than he had ever seen in his life. He was elated.

He calculated the amount he expected to receive from the sales based on the size of the farm and the number of bags he would fill. He spent much time thinking of all the things he would buy after he sold the harvest. He took all the bags he had, bought additional bags at the big market and placed them in a bundle on the ground. He then picked one stalk of rice and placed it in a bag before going home.

That night he was so anxious that he could neither sleep nor wait for daybreak. He arose very early, got ready and set out for his farm, dragging along his wife. He was tired with her drama. She complained all the time that it was too early. However, today, he paid her no mind as he was in a hurry to get there. He purposely ignored her whining.

Upon reaching the farm, he could not believe his eyes and shouted for his wife to hurry up. She had not been able to catch up with him since they left their home this morning. He had been running almost all the time whilst she took her time to get there. She figured, "The farm is not going anywhere, it will be sitting in the same place waiting for me so why rush?"

As she got closer to the farm, the sound of her husband's voice frightened her so much that she rushed over to him. She saw him sitting in the middle of the cleared area with his head between his knees. Carrying a calabash full of water, she hurried to him thinking he had fainted. She was ready to pour water on him to awaken him but she realized that he was alive. She was not surprised to see that he was in total shock.

She enquired what the matter was but he only turned and pointed with his hand for he was at a loss for words. It took her a while before she understood that he was indicating the place where he had left the bags the previous day. When she stood up and took in the sight she realized why he looked as if he had seen a ghost. The farmland had been wiped out. There were no bags, no rice stalks, nothing. It was as empty as the day they had cleared it after the burning.

Unable to grasp what had happened, he asked his wife, "Did you take away anything from the farm as you left yesterday?"

She said, "Not really. I didn't, except for the one stalk of rice that I put in a bag, along with the farm tools. What is the matter? What happened to all the rice? I do not understand where it had all gone. We left it all here."

He could barely speak as he sputtered, "You foolish woman, why did you do that?" He had feared that this might happen, so he had made sure to take every precaution against it. "What were you thinking on before you did that?"

She replied, "I was thinking that we would have had to carry all the bags of rice to town eventually so I was trying to save us the trouble. I thought that if I took the rice home in the bag, whatever or whoever was doing our farm work would bring the rice home to us, thus making our work easier."

What she did not know was that the forest spirits were only going to repeat an act performed on the farm. By taking the bag from the farm, she had given them their last instructions for the day. They simply came at night, filled up the bags with rice, and carried them off the farm as she had done. That was why they found nothing on the farm that morning.

The shame and disgrace was too much for the farmer to face. He was so angry that he began beating his wife, but she ran away. He then decided to wait until nightfall before he went home so that no one would see him enter the town without his harvest.

By late evening, he was so tired of doing nothing that he fell asleep under a tree. There he remained until night fell and the forest spirits came to the farm and beat him to death since it was the last thing he had done to his wife before she left the farm. Thus, the farmer died and the forest grew again on the land. No one ever farmed on the land again.

CHAPTER VI

The Fisherman's Wish

There was once a lonely angler who went forth daily on the river in his canoe and fish. He was clever and industrious. His name was Zarwolo. The clan's people considered him the best angler of all. None had his fishing skills. He could catch the largest sea animal or the smallest. He could provide the Chief's palace with any amount of fish they desired during a feast or major occasion.

However, Zarwolo had a secret. He was a lonely man. He had this great emptiness within, and whenever he was alone, he felt it the most. He knew that many of the young maidens adored him, but he suspected this was so because they knew he would be a good provider for them and their families. They did not really care for him, only what he could provide for them. He would often wish in his heart, "Ah, great Spirits, if I only had a wife my life would be so complete."

Unfortunately, the situation stayed the same, so the deeper he yearned for a woman who would love him. Over time, things got so bad that he began losing his interest in fishing. He reached to the point where he would have preferred a wife to all the fishes in the river. He was getting older and was lonelier than ever. He had no family nor a son to teach his trade to and carryon his name. Each day, despite his great catches and the joy he brought to others in the clan, he returned to an empty hut, prepared his own meals, and passed the night alone.

As he sits in his canoe fishing, he often prayed to the water spirits, "Great Water Spirits, you know how much I desire a wife, could you heed my wishes and grant me one. I promise to cherish her, love all our many children and train them properly. I will show more love than any man has ever shown is wife and family." He kept at it until on one of such occasions a River Spirit overheard him. She had the fern of a crocodile and lived on the bottom of the river. She took note and decided to keep an eye on Zarwolo. After a short while, it became clear to her that Zarwolo was gentle and honest man, but he was in too much sorrow.

One day, after Zarwolo had concluded his fishing, he hurried off to the main weekly market to sell his produce. The River Spirit waited until he had gone, then she climbed onto the riverbank in the form of a crocodile. She checked to make sure that no one was around. Convinced she was alone, she stepped out of the crocodile's skin. Beneath the skin was a spectacularly beautiful maiden. She found a secret place, hid her crocodile skin underneath a rock, and went to the big market.

She was not long in the market when she felt the stares the men gave her. Her beauty awed them. The women looked mostly out of envy than admiration. She was a talking point that day. They all wondered which village the pretty maiden came from.

At the end of the market day, she went to the angler's villages and as was the custom, she expected to spend the night. She presented herself to the chief's palace and requested to kindly spend the night. Nearly every man wanted to host her but they knew their wives would not take kindly to the idea, so the chief sent the stranger to the fisherman's house for the night.

Zarwolo received her with all courteousness. He asked her, "What would you like to eat so that I can prepare it? Do you have a favorite dish?"

She however interrupted him and informed him, "That is so kind of you, but as much as I appreciate this, it is not in line with my culture. Where I come from, it is the woman that prepares meals for the guests."

Thus, she begged that he allow her to do the favor in return for his kindness. She prepared him a simple meal like none other he had eaten before. At first, he ate out of hunger, and then he ate out of pure delight. He had never tasted such a nicely prepared dish. After that, they talked about themselves a little while before they slept. Zarwolo lie in bed thinking only of this pretty woman who could cook so well.

Early the next morning, the maiden asked him, "Zarwolo, could you please escort me some way on my journey? I do not wish to leave at day light. My road is far, therefore, the sooner I leave, the earlier I will arrive."

He did not hesitate. "Sure, I would be glad to do that." He also did not want to lose a moment with her.

A safe way out of the village, she requested, "I think this is far enough, why don't you leave me here. I can continue from here onward."

He protested, "No way, it is almost dawn and the forest could still be dangerous. Let me take you further."

However, she insisted. "It is not necessary. I really can make it on my own. Besides, don't you have work to do? The farther you go the longer your way back home would be. Just leave me here.

He was not happy with this but he obliged, "Okay." He said and they parted ways.

When she was sure she was safely alone, she went to the riverbank, and having carefully looked about, she slipped into the crocodile skin and went into the river'.

During the following days, the town was abuzz with Zarwolo's exploits. Each person, it seems, had their version of what might have transpired that night, but since Zarwolo did not indulge in such talks, they kept their gossips to themselves. None dared ask him for details.

Zarwolo kept up his routine. Each day he repeated his pleas to his Ancestors to return the beautiful maiden. All he spoke of was this maiden. The Water Spirit heard Zarwolo speak longingly for the lovely maiden who had passed the night within his house. He pleaded with the Water Spirits to have a wife like her. He was sure his happiness was in such a fair maiden. All this while, the Water Spirit kept listening to his pleas and devising a way to return for longer than one night.

On one big market day, the river spirit came out of the water again, hid her crocodile skin beneath the rock, and went to market. Again, she sought shelter at Zarwolo's place, and he was glad when he saw her. She prepared him another wonderful dish and passed the night. In the morning, she went away despite everything he tried to do.

This continued for some time and Zarwolo grew to love her a great deal. However, being a naturally shy man, he could not muster enough courage to ask her hand in marriage. He figured that such a maiden was a chief's daughter or that of another high-ranking member of the court and way out of his league. He would rather have her this way than to lose her, or so he led himself to believe. On their morning trips, he tried finding out where she came from in hopes of knowing for certain what he suspected. However, she never gave out much along those lines.

This, he told himself, would finally stop him from lusting after her. "Where do you live?"

"In a town not too far from here?" she replied.

"Like how close are we talking about? He pressed.

"Close enough for me to be here and see you."

"Are you with your family?

"Haha, do you think I fell of the sky Zarwolo?

"No I did not mean it like that."

"I know, I was just joking."

Often, this is how it was. She was always evasive when answering his questions about her family and home. With time, he grew suspicious of this attitude and decided to dig a little deeper. He had grown so fond of her that he was not going to take the easy way out, if the possibility existed for him to have her as a wife, he wanted to know and take it. If not, he needed to know and get over her as soon as possible.

There came a certain day when he escorted her and as usual, she requested, "Okay Zarwolo, you know the drill."

"Yeah, yeah. I shall leave you to continue your journey."

"Thank you, you always understand; that is something I like about you." She said.

He bid her farewell but this time around, he did not go home as he always did. When he was convinced that she could no longer see or hear him, he back tracked to the point and watched to see what she would do. His search led him along the riverbank. He got there just in time to see a huge crocodile enter the water, but nothing more. He waited a bit, but still no action in the area. It was as if she just vanished. After searching for a long time, he decided to be more tactful the next time.

The next market day came and they went through their motions and had a superb time. When he dropped her off, he immediately turned back retracing his steps, silently. This time he got there in time to see her search the rock near the bank and transform in to a crocodile. He could not believe his eyes. He was astonished, "Can this be true?" he thought to himself. "Is she, then a Water Spirit? How could I have fallen in love with one?"

Puzzled and deep in thought, Zarwolo went away, and plotted his next move. He loved her and he needed to find a solution to this situation. Whatever it was, he decided it had to be quick because the next market day the maiden would come and he had to be ready.

He went to the shrine priest and sought advice. "I have a problem I need your advice."

"What is your problem son?" The Diviner asked.

He explained his condition.

"Do you love her?" The Diviner asked.

"Yes, Great One. I find myself deeply in love with her. She makes me very happy even though she is a spirit being. I know this sounds crazy but it is the truth." He confessed

The Diviner warned him, "There are few things that can be done to help you, but each method is dangerous. I mean very dangerous.

"If you can help me please do, whatever it is just do it. I don't really care as long as we are together," he replied.

The Diviner said, "This is a most unusual situation and you have to be certain that you really want to go through with it. You are crossing the world of the spirit beings. There are dire consequences for any breech."

"I understand and still want to go through. Just make us to be together."

Thus, the Diviner went into trance and performed a ritual after which he gave Zarwolo a set of instructions. He had to follow to the letter any deviation would spell trouble.

Zarwolo listened keenly, paused as if in doubt, then asked him, "Could you go over them again to make sure I do not miss anything?"

"First, you are to find the crocodile skin and hide it. Doing this would break the connection between the two worlds." The Diviner began.

"Okay, I can do that." Zarwolo interrupted.

"She would not be able to transform again." The Diviner continued. "This will keep her in the human form she assumed."

"Good." Zarwolo muttered. This news pleased him greatly.

Secondly, the Shaman said, "She is never to see the skin again, if she did, her human form would die, any child of hers or anything associated with her will vanish, and she would return to the spirit world. Do you understand me?" The vigorous nod of Zarwolo was more than enough indication that he fully understood the dangerous nature of failing to live up to his end of his of the dear.

"Thirdly," the old man continued, "Under no circumstance should anyone else see the skin for that person will die as well. This cannot happen."

"Yes I understand." Zarwolo said.

"Fourthly, you are to clean the skin regularly to keep it in a perfect condition. You should also not let her enter into the river from the spot where she came out. The water from that part of the river can't touch her, if it does, she will disappear along with everything she has touched. Do you understand?" The old man asked.

"I do," was the only reply that came out.

"Lastly, every life requires a life in return. Are you willing to pay this price?" the Diviner stopped to stare at Zarwolo as he responded.

"Yes I am." He figured that since he had no family, he could outwit the old man. He would get his wife at no human cost. At least that is how he factored things. Over all, the deal was a good one for him.

Thus, after agreeing, the Diviner prepared the ritual and gave him some things to take along. He went home and waited for the next market day.

The day arrived and he was up earlier than usual and full of excitement. He rushed to the river and hid.

At dawn, the crocodile came on land, went into the surrounding bush and there it transformed into the beautiful maiden. She hid the skin under a rock and covered it with branches and leaves. She proceeded to the market. When Zarwolo was sure she had gone far, he removed the skin and hid it and continued with his fishing. He took his catch to the market, sold them, and met his maiden in the process.

They went about their usual routine and by morning when he left her at the spot, he was elated. He went on home this time for he knew what he had done. She searched the entire riverbank for the skin but did not find it. She was alarmed and kept frantically looking. However, she had to stop when other women came to fetch water and do their chores.

This she did each time she was alone, but still could not find the skin. Frustrated, she went to Zarwolo's place.

When he saw her, he feigned surprised and enquired, "What are you doing here? Is everything alright?"

"Yes all is well," was her reply. "I just miss you and came back to spend a little more time with you."

He was genuinely happy but noticing that she was worried made him somewhat sad. The whole night her mood was solemn. He tried comforting her but it did not seem to work.

Eventually, she settled down and told him, "I might have to stay a while longer, possible even move in this town. I like the place and want to be close to you." All of this was true but was not the real reason she came back.

After a few days, each of which she searched for her skin but never found it, Zarwolo asked her, "Will you marry me? I know I'm not wealthy or royalty, but I really love you and wish to make you happy?"

She was gladden by the news. "This makes me happy, but sadly, I cannot accept your offer. I do not think it is fair to you. I wish I could explain but I can't."

"Whatever it is, you can tell me." He said, whilst holding her hand.

"I can't. It is not easy to do."

"Try me I can handle it. Is it your family?

"No, it is not." She replied.

"Is it a husband? Are you betrothed to another person? Is it because I am not rich?" he pressed on.

"No, it is not any of those things." She fired back with a trace of anger. "Why would you think like that about me? Do you think I care about money? If I did, would I be here with you?"

"I am sorry my dear." He paused before pulling her closer. "Do you love me? I need to know this. Is it because you do not love me?"

She turned slowly, cupped his face and said, "I love you. In fact, I have never loved like this before. Do not ever doubt that because it will hurt me."

"Well then why not marry me? In fact, I am willing to go to your parents now and ask your hand in marriage. Let us go, now. I am not afraid to ask."

"I do not have parents. I am alone." She said and dropped her head.

She remained looking at the ground until he held her chin, caressed it small and lifted her head. He stared her in the eyes and said, "You are not alone. You never are, not as long as I live. I am here for you and will stay by your side no matter what the situation is." He pulled her closer to him and cuddled her, tight at first, then gradually released the pressure.

They embraced for a while, she pulled away and said, "The truth is, when you love someone, you try to protect them and not hurt them. Things could only go bad for all of us if I stayed. What I need now is your understanding. I know it is difficult but please try. Just let things be this way for a while and let me sort out a few things. Can you do that for us please?" she pleaded.

"Just give me one good reason why you think this way." He asked.

"Let me confess, I do not belong here. I come from a place far off and could not return until I settled some things. I need you to understand. Where I come from things are different than here."

All this time, he pretended not to know what the issue was but he was sad she was going through such pain. "Okay, I will give you time to sort things out. In the meantime, I wish you to know this; I'll be good to her forever when we are married."

She sighed and kissed him. "Thank you so much, you do not know how much this means to me. I promise not to forget it."

She searched every opportunity she got but failed to find the skin. With time, she came to accept that she might not find the skin at all so she agreed to marry him reluctantly. She feared that someone might find the skin, and this she knew was a bad thing.

Time went by and she could not get any children. She tried not to have any because she still had her fears, but eventually she gave birth to a boy. That night much feasting went on. The angler gave away free fish to almost everyone who wanted. He held a party for his wife and new kid. At the end of the occasion when everyone had gone home, the spirit of the underworld appeared to him and told him to choose between his baby and his wife. One had to die as per agreed upon, a life for a life. Zarwolo pleaded but to no avail. The Spirit insisted, he even offered his life in exchange but the Underworld Spirit refused.

Zarwolo had to choose, his wife or his newborn baby. He could have only one. In the end, he realized that he could not trick the Diviner after all. Whom will he choose?

CHAPTER VII

The Hunter's Dilemma

Misters Dog, Eagle and Otter were three inseparable friends. They loved the forest. They hunted, played and even lived together for many years. As they grew older, they started thinking about getting married and having a families. They all promised to be friends forever and to raise their children to be friends.

One day, as they were out playing, they came across a maiden on her way to fetch water. She was so pretty that each of them stood in their tracks, and none dared move. The noise of the other maidens on the way to the creek snapped them out of their trance and they all ran into hiding. They then followed the girls to the creek but remained hidden in the bushes.

Each day, at around the same time, they would go out on the road to the creek and watch the maiden. Soon, her friends noticed and teased her about it. "Somebody has a crush."

"What crush?" asked the maiden.

"Don't you mean several crushes?" Another teased.

She insisted, "You guys are crazy. There is nothing going on here. It is nothing to it but your imagination."

With time, they got comfortable enough to ask her name and began visiting her. Just when all was going well, Mr. Otter decided to make a move. He called his friends together that morning and informed them, "I intend to seek the maiden's hand in marriage and appealed for your support when I ask her parents this evening." This was shocking news to them.

"What are you talking about? Why would you want to do this when you know very well that it is I the maiden gazes on with longing?" asked Mr. Eagle. "She looks up at me and blows kisses." Mr. Eagle said.

Mr. Dog barked in anger. "What kind of foolishness is this? Each day we come here, who does the maiden stroke tenderly? Who does she and her friends kneel down and play with?" asked the dog.

Each in turn related how the maiden had actually made gestures toward him and that the other should not dare. A fight broke out between them. No one seemed willing to listen to the other nor did anyone seem ready to back down.

The next few days got worse. Each animal went to the maiden's house. The first was the dog. He asked the mother, "Oldma, you like me right?"

She seemed taken aback by the question but did not hesitate to say, "Of course, I do. Who does not like a nice fluffy companion like you?"

"Good," said Mr. Dog.

"Why are you asking?" the maiden's mother inquired.

"Nothing oh," said the dog, "I just wanted to be sure."

"Mr. Dog," the woman said, looking at him with a look of one who knows better, "You know that you can't fool me right? What is going on here?"

"Well," he hesitated, and then spoke. "I was wondering. I really like you and your family. I was thinking that now that your daughter is of age, if you would help me talk to your husband on my behalf. I really love her and want her hand in marriage. You know I am hard working and will make a good son in law. In fact, I will even help him hunt more meat which we could sell and get money to buy many other things. I will take the best care of your daughter; more than anyone else would"

"Oh, this is what this is about?" the woman asked. "Anyway, I hear you and I promise to tell my husband at the right time. We will see what he has to say. This is a delicate matter so we must do so at the right time."

Thus, they continued doing what they were doing and discussed the subject no more.

Early the next morning, when the husband left to hunt, Mr. Eagle, flew in. He knew that Mr. Dog had tagged along with the hunter in pretense of helping catch game. He really was trying to win the man's favor. He on the other hand, had his plans. He perched on the roof and scanned the area, once satisfied, he came to the kitchen window and said, "Good morning Oldma, how are you today?"

"I am fine oh and you?" The mother replied.

"I am doing well. Anyways I just came by to greet you and gave you a small gift," he dropped the monkey he had snatched on the floor as he said this.

"Oh thank you," the woman said. "You know what? Why don't you just wait around while I prepare some hot pepper soup with this meat? We can be lecturing until the chew is ready."

Thus, they talked and eventually, Mr. Eagle came around to his purpose. He explained why he believed himself the best person to marry the maiden. She made no promise other than to talk to her husband upon his return.

They ate their food in silence and the eagle flew off afterwards.

Later that evening, the maidens accompanied her mother to the creek to fetch water. She and the other girls ran ahead to gossip and talk about boys out of the hearing of their mothers. As the mother was removing her bucket from the water, Mr. Otto surfaced. "My Oldma, how is your evening? Is everything alright?"

"Yes my son, everything is fine. What about you? Are you doing well?" she asked.

"I'm okay," he replied. They talked for a while as she collected her water. Just when she was about to leave, he told her to wait. He dived into the water and after a few moments, he returned and said, "Here is something for you." He gave her a big catfish.

"Thank you," she said, and as before, she offered to prepare an evening meal and share with him. They went home and talked along the way. In time, he came around to ask the mother for her daughter's hand. He thought he made a convincing case.

"You know this is not up to me to make that decision, but I will tell my husband when he returns. That settled the issue for the time being.

Thus, all three of them played their cards as they awaited the husband's reply. None, however, dared ask the father directly. They all feared that as a hunter, he might not hesitate to pull out his gun and shoot them. Each figured that the wife was best person to make a convincing case for him.

Meanwhile, the maiden and her friends noticed that the three were no longer together. Instead, each came to the creek alone and tried to win her affection. This seemed strange since they were deliberately avoiding each other. However, the charade did not last as some bad news interrupted it.

They learned that the hunter failed to return home. The news spread throughout the town. Such an important hunter was invaluable to the town and the chief was rightly concerned. As was traditional in the town, well-wishers went by to comfort the family. The animals also joined in wishing the family well.

The mother was overwhelmed with everything. When she saw the three hovering nearby a three in their yard, she had a thought. She called them aside and said. "The one who finds my husband and brings him back alive will marry my daughter." They were surprised, but accepted the challenge.

When they left the house, Mr. Eagle suggested, "You know what? I think that we should work together. We have been friends from childhood and should not forget that. To be honest, we work better as a team. I am sure you will all agree that cooperating on issues has helped us in the past and should do so now."

"I think you are right," Mr. Otto said.

"Yes, I also agree," said the dog. "In fact, I think I should take the lead. No one sniffs better than I do." Thus, Mr. Dog took the lead. He smelt and sniffed until he picked up the scent of the hunter. They followed it until they reached the riverbank. Then he lifted his head and informed them, "This is where it ends, right here. I think he must have gone into the water. Beyond this point, I am not sure we can track him, we have to find another means."

They all stood there thinking the same thing but each afraid to say it out. This particular water was the dwelling place of the Water People. Everyone in the land knew this. They also feared the Water People because once they got hold of you they didn't let go. With the trail ending here, it appeared all hope was gone.

However, Mr. Otter said, "I will have to pay them a visit. They are my friends from long ago. The least we can do is try." With this, he dived into the water and swam down into the depths. When he got there, he heard loud drum rolls and saw that a noisy festival was going on. Before he could enquire as to the cause of the celebration, he saw the hunter tied to a stick. They lit a huge bonfire and water people were arriving from all over.

He rushed to the Water King and after paying his respects, pleaded. "My wise old friend, could you please stay the slaying of the hunter? He is a good man."

The King was curious for this was an odd request. "My good friend, why would I do such a thing? It has been a long time since me and my people had a decent meal, so why should we give this one up?"

"The hunter is my friend. I'd rather you didn't eat him," said Mr. Otter.

The Water Chief shook his head slowly. He informed him, "You know very well that things have been rough on us lately. This man is partly responsible for the hardship we are experiencing.

Mr. Otter was surprised, and asked, "How is that so?"

"He has driven away the monkeys that used to frequent our water. At least when they did, we grabbed some and feasted on them. Now it is impossible to get hold of a single monkey."

Mr. Otter paused, and suggested, "Why don't you people eat catfish and tilapia like the others?"

The Chief replied, "That is all we get to eat, you know that. We can't live well only on fish. Furthermore, we are just tired of fish. It is not as if we have other options, the fact is, fish is all that is left since man decided to destroy the forest and drive the animals away. Hunters are the worst of men."

Mr. Otter tried every trick available. He did his best to make his friends release the hunter but each time the chief return a negative response. Almost discouraged, he suggested a trade. "How about I find you a hundred raccoons and possums, some rice and a barrel of fresh palm oil? Would you let the hunter go free?"

The Water Chief turned slowly to his friend and said, "No trade, we want this man."

"You are not a bad king, and I understand your situation, but at least think about it," said Mr. Otto.

The king paused and after rolling the thought over he said, "I know you are trying to save your friend so I will try and help you. The only trade we will consider is one hundred monkeys, that or the hunter dies."

Mr. Otter realized that nothing would get the hunter out of there except finding them the monkeys. He also knew that he was running out of time. The sooner he got the monkeys there the better. However, there was one problem with the idea. It was nearly impossible to catch so many monkeys under the present conditions. In fact, catching one was difficult enough, so how would they catch one hundred! The monkeys were simply too fast. They leaped and jumped from branch to branch at alarming speed.

When he got to the surface, Mr. Otter met his two anxious friends who feared the Water People had eaten him. They were relieved to see him, but sad not to see the hunter. He told them the demands of the Water People.

"What!" screamed the dog. "Are they crazy? There is no way to catch so many monkeys. They might as well kill him."

Mr. Eagle pondered for a while and suggested he talk to his friends. With that, he flew off. He contacted all the eagles he knew and asked them to help him get his bride. They in turn, asked other eagles and soon the monkey kingdom was on fire. Eagles of every kind swarmed in on them. They captured as many monkeys possible but did not reach one hundred. Therefore, they flew off again and managed to get the number. They dropped them into the water and flew off.

The Water People were stunned at first, then overwhelmed. Every few moments, they would drop a monkey into the water. When they counted one hundred, the Chief ordered the hunter released. Mr. Otter collected him and they returned to the surface.

Now they all went back to the hunter's house. There was much rejoicing and fanfare. When he settled down, his wife informed him of the promise she made to the animals. She said, "You should now give your daughter's hand in marriage to the one who had brought him back safely."

At first, he had been grateful to Mr. Otter, but when he got to the land, he learned that Mr. Dog's keen sense of smell was the only thing that led them to the river. Mr. Otter's friendship with the Water People had made it possible for him to negotiate his terms of release, and the courage of Mr. Eagle and his friends had secured his ransom. Thus, he was alive today because of all of these efforts. The question now was to which one should he give his daughter's hand in marriage?

CHAPTER VIII

How Fire came to Earth

Maleka, the God who dwells in the sky, decided to visit his creation. During his visit, he observed that things were going well with them. On his way back, Maleka noticed that some stars were dark and others were running out of light. He decided to fix the problem when he returned. He called the hawk and instructed it, "Mr. Hawk, I want you to perform a task for me."

"Sure, Maleka, anything you wish." He replied.

"I want you to rekindle the burnt out stars and to revive the dying ones. For this task, I will trust you with something very important." He gave the hawk a stick of fire as he spoke. "You know that fire was one of the things I did not give to mankind after creation.

I thought it appropriate to keep man and fire apart. I thought that the destructive natures of man and fire were too potent to mix. I feared that real trouble could ensue if these two were enemies. Therefore, take particular care Mr. Hawk not to go anywhere near earth. I know that the you like to play around the villages and grab a chicken or two. However, this time you are not to go near the place until you have done this work. Do you understand?"

"Yes I do. I promised that I would finish this task and report here before I go anywhere near the villages to eat or play."

Mr. Fire on the other hand was not too happy to be trusted with the hawk. He felt too proud after dwelling too long with Maleka. "Maleka, I do not feel comfortable with this arrangement. This is nothing short of embarrassing. I feel like I have wronged you wish to punish me. It is not proper that I should have to mix with the likes of Mr. Hawk."

"Why would you say that Mr. Fire?" enquired the hawk. You are too proud and act as if you are better than others."

"How can we be compared? I dwell up here with Maleka and other nobilities. You on the other hand, belong down there with the other lower class animals," said the fire.

He protested to Maleka. "Can't you find another way?"

"Maleka I will do the task correctly. I am the best person for the job." Mr. Hawk injected.

"What! You? Best person? Maleka, at least you could try something else. In fact, why don't you take me along on your next visit Maleka? That way, you could rekindle the stars yourself. That is much better."

"I am afraid Mr. Fire that is not an option. We do not have time. This can't wait." Maleka explained. "There is an urgency to relight the stars. It would benefit many others in the universe."

"Well, if that is the case, at least entrust me with someone else that did not frequent the earth and played foolish plays."

In the end, he did not succeed in convincing Maleka so he had to go with the hawk. On the way, Mr. Hawk tried to convince with fire that he was responsible enough to perform the task. "I am the best person for this job. I am fast and have a steady grip."

"You are not." Mr. Fire disagreed. "You are irresponsible and belong to this pitiful world."

"Who are you calling irresponsible Mr. Fire? What have you done since your creation? You have no children, no feelings; you are just sitting up there paying lip service to Maleka. The fact that I am of this world is even more reason I should be taking you. I know my way around."

This back and forth continued for a while and eventually turned into a full disagreement between the two. Mr. Hawk felt insulted and told him so. In the ensuing argument, the hawk had subconsciously flown too close to earth since this was his usual route. None of them noticed this for they were busy arguing. When Mr. Fire said a particularly nasty thing to the hawk, he attempted to respond in like manner so he shouted. "You are very selfish and foolish. You are a good for nothing bigot; a useless object just occupying space."

"How dare you, you ignorant flying creature?" Mr. Fire shot back.

Unfortunately, in his anger, Mr. Fire began to get hot; this made Mr. Hawk to drop him in the process. He dove towards the earth attempting to grasp the falling fire. Mr. Fire was furious and as he continued his barrage of insults, he burned hotter. He did not make it easy for Mr. Hawk to hold him. In fact, he thought that the hawk was trying to rip him apart with his claws and beak so he resisted each attempt to catch him before his fall. They kept at this, shouting insults and threats at one another until Mr. Fire fell to the earth.

He landed in a pile of leaves and wood the kids had piled up and were playing around. The angry fire could not believe it. He did not have time to consider his new surrounds when he noticed that a bunch of funny looking creatures surrounded him. The excited kids screamed and some rushed to touch him, enraging him even more. Soon, other strange creatures came rushing at him, they were bigger versions of the little ones that first attempted to touch him. The crowd grew and they were suffocating him. He got enraged the more, burned faster, and hotter.

The onlookers were amazed. They could not phantom the concept of fire. He had glowing lights of different colors, which was beautiful to their eyes. He was fast and he produced heat and warmth. Some kids were too excited that they ran and held Mr. Fire. In response, he burnt them. They went screaming in pain, which enraged their parents. They threw stones at him, but this only infuriated him. He blazed more. They threw grass and sticks at him but this just fed him and filled him with anger. He despised man and did not appreciate the way they treated him in such a low manner. They tried almost everything to stop Mr. Fire but nothing seemed to work. They began to fear him because he ate everything in his path. Mr. Hawk tried in vain to recover him from the black and grey smoke he was emitting.

He went on damaging everything in his path. It seems the harder the people tried to stop him, the more the fire raged. Finally, he came to a house and engulfed the kitchen. The woman who was doing her chores had nothing in her hand but a pail of water. In a desperate attempt to save her house from burning, she threw it at him. All the people were shouting at her from a distance to leave the house and run to safety.

However, when they arrived, they were shocked. They saw her repeatedly pour water at Mr. Fire and each time she did that it calmed him no matter how enraged he was. He would hiss loudly and blow off a lot of steam, but will go off in the end. In their astonishment, they forgot to help her. She had to scream at them, "You foolish people! Get more water and help me. Go and fetch more water!"

Eventually, they joined her and added more water, each time they succeeded in quenching Mr. Fire's anger some more. When they had almost subdued the fire, an elder forced his way through and yelled, "Stop! Stop it right now! Let us not kill it, we must save this animal."

"Are you mad or something?" a woman whose child the fire had burnt asked him.

"Be careful how you speak to me." The man snapped.

They all looked back and realized that this was the oldest man of the community. "I am sorry." The woman apologized. "But this is a monster. We can't allow it to live."

"Yes we can't," another mother chimed in. "Look at how much destruction it has caused us?"

"It burned my whole hut down." Another said.

"It damaged my entire farm, now I have nothing to eat or sell," said a farmer.

It nearly killed my child and several other children of this community, so why should we allow it to live?" An angry mother yelled.

"I know that this creature has caused so much damage in a short time, but you all are not thinking strait. Imagine having this animal as a friend."

"What friend? No one can be friends with a monster." The hunter blurted out.

"You must think of the future. We must try to understand it and appease it. Maybe with time, we could be friends, but if not, we still know how to kill it. Therefore, if it becomes too much of a problem, we already have a solution." The elder reasoned.

"Hmm." It makes sense, another elder said.

"Think. With this monster, we can surprise the lions and tigers that eat our children. We could kill the bears and leopards that terrorize our community. They do not know we have it, but when they come, we can finally get our revenge and keep them away from us forever. This new animal may be a monster, but it can help protect us from other dangerous animals. It can help keep us safe."

As he was convincing them, Mr. Hawk manages to dash down and scoops up the almost calm Mr. Fire and flies away.

"Quick! Stop the hawk!" yelled the elders.

The men rushed to protect the fire since they all knew what the hawk did to its victims. They threw stones and sticks at Mr. Hawk. As he dodged these objects, some fire fell to the ground again. The men managed recover it and take it to the elders.

Mr. Hawk rushed to the dying stars and began rekindling them one after the other. Few had died because their fires went out. He was able to complete the job, but not before losing some of the fire to man. He now had a huge problem. He used all the fire he had scooped up to save the stars. He could not return to Maleka without Mr. Fire. He was afraid that Maleka would punish him for his error. He needed to carry some fire back with him. He decided not to return to the heavens until he succeeded in freeing

Mr. Fire from the human race. This was the only part of fire left and man was protecting it.

It is for this reason Mr. Hawk scouts every village and town of man in search of fire. At times, he even takes chickens and other domesticated animals of man just to punish them. His task is harder since Mr. Fire is still mad at him and still refuses to allow Mr. Hawk to touch him. Each time Mr. Hawk gets close enough to hold Mr. Fire, it makes the fire angry and he burns fiercely.

Thus, it was that man saved Mr. Fire, but only to be a prisoner to them. Man kept him away from hawk and with time, man mastered how to use the fire. The women learned the magic of fire and they cooked their food, heated their water and did other things with it. Men learned how to mold iron and other things with fire, but man has never given him his freedom for fear that he may revenge his captivity.

CHAPTER IX

The Wisest will be King

Long ago in Liberia, there lived a great king. He ruled for many years and had won many battles. He was a fierce warrior but a good man. He built his kingdom into the most powerful in the world and every major empire in the world respected him.

One day he decided to host a feast in honor of his rule. He invited every major royalty from every part of the world. This was the feast of the century and everyone that mattered wanted to be there. Animals from every corner of the earth traveled to Liberia to celebrate this great king's rule. The food and meat were plentiful. Even the ants had enough stored away for rainy days. As for the drinks, it came in calabash and barrels. There was sweet cane juice, palm wine, bitterroots and many more. Those fond of the bottle drank from morning to night, with many passing out several times over. Everyone was merry except the great chief. He alone knew the real reason for this grand feast.

On the last day of the feast, as everyone gathered around as per the chief's request, he broke the news, "I am glad that you all came to celebrate with me, this is a very special moment for me. I thank you for making it so, but that this would be my last time celebrating with you my friends. I have nothing but fond and happy memories of my time in life."

Mr. Owl let out several hoots, "Hoooo, Whooooo, Hwooooo!"

Sadly, he said, "However, my time has come and I will soon be departing this world to be with the great spirits and my ancestors. I have but one request; choose a successor from amongst you to continue where I stop. Let it be one who will lead with wisdom and compassion"

This news was just too much for them to bear. Many wailed and pleaded with the good king for some way to intercede on his behalf. Mr. Dog lamented. "Oh great and mighty King, you have no equal. In all my years, I have met none that comes even close to you. I consider none a better chief, father, ruler or friend than you Great Chief. In fact, I fear that upon your demise our great kingdom would cease to exist." The king consoled him, assuring him that no such thing would happen.

As this sad moment was occurring, three very strange and old looking animals entered the court. No one seemed to know who they were or from whence they had come. The entire court fell silent upon seeing these strangers. They advanced slowly towards the mighty Chief and paid their respect.

"Oh great and powerful Chief, who can replace you? Certainly no one," said the first one and he continued his platitudes.

The second one kneeled down as well when he spoke, "Mighty Chief, news of your kindness travels far and wide. We are here certainly because of them."

The last stranger prostrated and spoke with face lowered, "Powerful chief, as you know, we barely leave our abodes, but for this occasion, we did in testament of the high regards in which we hold you."

The Chief remembered that his parents told him the story of how some strangers visited their kingdom long ago when there was hardship and war and how their wisdom helped their ancestors to form this kingdom out of the endless tribal wars. He assumed these were the same ones but he made no mention of this. He simply invited them to sit in the area reserved for the most noble.

After a while, as if on cue the animals began to whisper and murmur. The foremost thing now seemed to be the identity of these three strangers. Mr. Spider said, "I am sure these are the messengers from the land of the spirits. They have come to take the Chief away."

"No they are not," said Mr. Rabbit. "They are incarnations of the great spirits and our ancestors. In the end, no one really knew who these men were.

The king interrupted their guessing games reminding them to, "Please break up into groups and decided who the next leader should be."

The younger animals soon pooled around and began plotting on whom they would select and how they would select that person. "We must make sure none of those old animals rule us again oh. They are hard to die, by the time one moves from there, we will all be old," said Mr. Spider.

"You are foolish," responded Mr. Fly. "Since when did you become our spokesman? It is better we put the old people there."

"I agree," said Mr. Rabbit, "they have wisdom and know how to lead."

Mr. Goat chimed in, "Me pah, I think it is time for young people to lead too. I agree with Mr. Spider." This broke into a yelling match in no time. They could not seem to agree on anything.

Meanwhile, the older animals on the other hand had much success with this. They did not know whom to select but they were not fighting like the younger ones. Mr. Owl spoke, "I do not know who to select but I suggest that we should all try to vote for the one who proved to be the oldest and wisest of us all. Thus, if anyone believes s/he is the oldest and wisest, then s/he should come forward and prove his or her case." This idea seemed agreeable to all, therefore they opened up the floor for candidates to justify their case. This went on smoothly as candidate of the other stepped forward and made their case.

Not surprisingly, Mr. Spider Sr. stepped up, "I am the wisest and oldest animal amongst you all. I have so many children that I cannot even count them. I have been living for so long until my waist has shrunk inward." Somehow, this did not convince the others, they dismissed his claim.

Next were Misters Rabbit and Monkey. "I am the one who is oldest therefore I should be the leader. I have lived so long, all my furs are grey.my ears are all sagging due to the many years they have seen." The group dismissed him as well.

"It is I who should make any meaningful claim to be Chief here," the older monkey said. "It is true that you have many children Mr. Spider, but it is not because you are the oldest. You just lay too many eggs and love woman business. As for you Mr. Rabbit, your fur is grey because that is the real color. Furthermore, you are not the wisest, if anything you may be the most crooked."

"It is true!" yelled Mr. Mosquito.

"But I am both wise and old," continued Mr. Monkey. "I am the one closest to human shape and thought, so I should be king. Who else resembles or thinks like humans?"

Mr. Baboon jumped in, "I do. I am even more alike humans than you are."

"But you are not smart, no hard feelings. I am just saying the truth," said the Fox.

"I don't want to be king, Mr. Fox. I was only correcting Mr. Monkey," said Mr. Baboon. This went on until they disqualified all interested candidates.

Surprisingly though, the three strangers stepped forward to lay claim to the throne. This gestured gained so much attention from all the animals gathered. Each of the three made a convincing case, in the end the animals could not decide who to lead. Therefore, they made the decision that a panel of judges along with the king should make the final selection.

After they decided on this, they hurriedly sent a message to the king that they had reached a decision on is successor. The chief dispatched the Town Crier to gather all the other animals. At the meeting, they presented the three strangers to the king saying that they would like to choose their new king from this short list of three. The king was as surprised but he tried to hide it. He invited the three strangers to step forward and present their cases.

The first up introduced himself as Mr. Toad. "I thank the king and his court for the opportunity to make my case. I also thank the other animals for granting me the chance to show that I am the best person for this job. I promise to rule effectively if selected." Turning to the judges, Mr. Toad continued.

"I'll be the new chief!" croaked Mr. Toad. "I'm the oldest, of the oldest! I have lived since the beginning of time! It is obvious that I should be the new chief," Mr. Toad declared in a croaky voice. "Even the sound of my voice can tell you that."

"Uhm," said one animal.

"Now let me tell you why I must be selected as the new king. I am older than my two colleagues are. I am so old I knew the world when it was formed. I lived in the world when it was pimpled all over with little hills. Between the hills were holes where evil spirits dwelt, therefore any living thing had to jump from hill to hill in order to avoid the spirit- holes, I was the only living thing, and that is how I learned to jump. As you can see, I still jump like that up till present time."

Everyone jumped up clapping and talking amongst themselves. There was much commotion.

Mr. Goat raised his voice loudly saying great king, "Truly, Mr. Toad is the most ancient of animals and must be our new chief. He has made a good case." His colleagues followed suit with even louder noise clapping harder and banging on anything they could find.

The Great Chief had to raise his hand for silence, which took some time before the room quieted down. "My people let us be patient and allow the other two animals to speak as well." After some grumbling, they grudgingly obeyed.

Next up on stage was an odd-looking animal encased in a shell. "I am Mr. Snail. I would like to thank the great chief and audience for the chance given me. I wish to make this clear from the beginning. I have no illusions of replacing your great leader for no one could live up to his record. Nevertheless, I only wish to be a good leader, if you would allow me to be your king." This seemed to strike a good cord with many of the animals present.

"I'm sure I'll be the new chief!" Mr. Snail whispered in a hoarse voice. The animals had to strain to hear him for his voice was so low.

"I am so old that my voice is frail. I have been speaking longer than any other animal alive, which is why I speak like this now. I am the oldest of the aged animals around. I was around way before the beginning of time. I was around at a time when Mr. Toad and my other colleague were not alive. I used to be so lonely and had no friends to play with."

"Wow," whispered a young raccoon.

He continued, "When the world was still a ball of soft mud, with-out hills or holes or anything else, I was around. No animal with legs could live in the world at that time. The only way to move was by sliding slowly on one's slimy belly. Because there was so much mud that was the way, my family and I managed to move around. The proof is in the way I moved, and still do. No other creature lived when I was young,"

A deafening noise emanated from the chief's Palace as the animals cheered and hooted. Mr. Sheep jumped up and down. Finally, he managed to raise his voice over the others. "My mighty king," he said, "Here indeed is the oldest animal in the whole world. For most certainly, Mr. Snail has proven his case and he must be our chief! We need not waste our time on the matter anymore. Let the celebrations begin. Let the palm wine and cane juice flow. We now have a new king."

Most of the younger animals seemed in agreement with this suggestion but Mr. Owl, on behalf of the judges pleaded, "My people please have your seats and just hear out the last of the three." They complained and protested until the king demanded their silence.

The last of the three struggled to get on the floor. He raised his wing for silence, and announced in the guttural voice that comes only with aging. "My name is Mr. Hornbill."

"What!" yelled Mr. Squirrel. "We can't hear you!"

"I am no skilled public speaker like my other colleagues, but I am honest and wise. I am certainly the most ancient of all animals alive today."

"Papay you have to speak louder," some youngsters shouted at him.

"Please bear with me," he pleaded. "Just be quiet and listen keenly. Age has taken away my voice a proof that I am the oldest alive, therefore I should claim the title of ruler. I deserve to be the new chief. I was old before time was made."

"Papay please talk the truth oh!" said Ms. Hen.

"Of a truth, I am much older than either Mr. Toad or Mr. Snail. I was born before the world began. When I was a child, there was no mud to slide over, no hills to hop onto and no holes to jump-over. The only animals alive were Hornbills and they caught their food as they flew about the sky. Things were flying around the air or in the water. Moreover, there was not even land for trees to grow on or for hornbills to bury their loved ones. If a hornbill died, we buried him or her in the beak of a family member, for there was no other place to bury the person. You see my beak?"

"Yeah what?" Ms. Pig said, as others turned to look.

He asked again, "Do you see how big it is?"

"Uh um," crooked Mr. Frog as several nodded.

"This is the coffin of his beloved mother!"

A chorus of "Wow," rang out as they all gasped. It appeared that he had proved his point. The ground shook like an earthquake and even the king could not calm the group as a bunch of youngsters they lifted Mr. Hornbill chanting "Long Live the King! Long Live the King!" The fact was evident, and the animals clapped and cheered, Mr. Hornbill proved himself the oldest creature in the world. They crowned him the new chief.

CHAPTER X

The Suitor's Dilemma

There once lived three brothers. They were extremely poor. The house they lived in was falling apart on them. Their parents were farmers but the land was so hard to yield that they had died in poverty despite their hard work. They did not know that a powerful shaman cursed the land long ago. All the brothers had was the old house and the cursed land.

No longer able to endure this hardship, the youngest brother, Paye, called his brothers together and asked them, "I think we need to think about our future, don't you? We are working harder each year and things are not getting any better. I fear if we do not do something drastic, we all risk living and dying on this farm just like our parents. I do not wish to spend my entire life working hard all in vain because the land would not produce. We have tried since our youth and the results are the same."

"It is true what you say," said Saye, his eldest brother. I also do want to end my life like this and wish that we could do something about it, but we can't."

"Oh we can, you just are not thinking about it that way," said Paye.

"As difficult as it is, we must keep trying. We have no other option, unless of course you had a better idea. Do you have a plan?" asked Saye.

"I do," replied Paye.

"Okay what is it? Speak!" Saye said.

"I think we should that we go to the Chief's palace and offer ourselves as royal servants. In exchange, we ask him to grant us three requests. We would each ask for anything we desire for a whole week after which we will work for him. To me, this is better than staying in the old house or farming on a land that produces nothing."

"This is crazy," said the Saye.

Nyahn spoke for the first time and he wasn't so quick to agree with him. "I think the pekin has a point."

"What! You can't be seriously agreeing to this foolishness." Paye raged.

"Think about it, what do we have to lose? Already as it is, we are getting nothing. Why don't we enjoy for once in our lives?" reasoned Nyahn.

"You call giving your freedom away enjoyment? How is that so?" asked Saye.

"First, we will eat nicely on a daily basis. We will get a decent place to lay our heads that is not leaking when it rains. We will get clothes and still, if we are lucky, we will be able to earn money. Oh not to forget the many beautiful maidens. If we are lucky, we will get some of them to like us."

However, after much argument, they agreed to try this crazy idea. They set off for the palace early the day after their decision. They had little, so packing for the trip was fast. The only problem was they were hungry and thirsty since they had no food. However, they picked food from some farms along the way and ate. They traveled on for several days. Eventually, they made it.

Upon arrival, they were welcome and granted an audience with the chief. He offered them his hospitality. They showered and returned to the court where he offered them food. They ate as if they never seen food before. When they finished, he sent them off to rest. He made sure they had more palm wine and food and a decent house to pass the night. This was the custom of the town; they treated strangers well upon arrival. They would discuss business tomorrow.

The next day, he asked, "What is it you seek in our town? Is it business or are you just passing through?"

Paye spoke for the group. "I thank you for your kindness towards me and my brothers. The truth is, what we seek is of a strange nature. All I can hope is that you can find it in your kind heart to consider our proposal to you."

"Well, say your piece," said the chief.

"We come from the edge of this great chiefdom. We are all that is left of our family. Our parents were farmers who worked hard all their lives and died poor. The only thing they left us was an old hut, which is barely fit for animals. The land is so dry and hard to toil. Imagine three grown men toiling the soil every season, yet to no avail. No matter how we water it, it still does not yield crops. In short, we are tired. More so, we are desperate. We wish to have some small measure of happiness before we die. Thus, we are pleading that you allow us to be palace servants for your court. We are hardworking and I promise we will not disappoint you.

"This is really a strange request," said the chief. "I have heard many requests, but this tops it all. "Normally, people who are free do not ask to be servants."

"We know this is not a usual request chief, but we have no other options," spoke Paye for the first time.

"What do you wish in exchange for this service, if I were to grant you it?" asked the chief.

After a pause, Saye spoke out, "We wish one request each. We would each ask for one thing for a week after which we will become your palace servants. Just one week of happiness is all we seek. At least we will know what it is like to be happy in life."

The chief pondered this for a while and finally he said, "I am sorry about your condition, but what you have proposed is something I must be sure you wish to do."

"We are," interrupted Paye.

"Very well," said the chief, "I will consult with my elders and get back to you. For now, you are free to stay here as my guests. Maybe you would change your minds before we get an answer for you." With this, he dismissed them.

When the chief arrived at an answer, he summoned the brothers. He said, "I want to know, are you certain about this? Have you changed your mind yet?"

"Yes sir, we are certain we want to go through with it. We have not changed our minds." Said Paye as Saye and Nyahn nodded agreement. The time here was better than any they had had. They figured that one week of this was worth it.

"Well, I must admit, you are a determined group of men."

"Yes we are, Chief. We wish this," said Paye.

Reluctantly, the chief agreed, not because he wished it but because it was customary to grant a stranger's request as long as it was within reason and the person wished it. In this case, the brothers insisted. The Chief asked, "So, what is it you desire? Take your time and think this through, when you have an answer let me know"

"We already have our answers," one replied.

"Oh really!" The chief and his council seemed rather surprised. "You seem to have put much thought in this. Anyways, let us hear it. Just speak. What is it you desire so badly for a whole week?"

Paye came forward and said, "Great Chief, I wish to have the finest palm wine in the entire palace. I have tasted wine before, but never have I tasted the kind you offered us along with the meal." He figured that he would get food and a resting place already as a guest, but he was not getting anywhere near the amount of wine he desired.

The Chief was surprised and he showed it. In fact, he was unsure if he heard him well. "Wine you said?" he asked to be sure. It was no secret that his chiefdom had the best wine tappers in all the land. However, wine seemed a strange request to him. "Are you certain of this, that this is what you wish?"

"Yes, chief, this is what I want, replied Saye.

The Chief then ordered the best palm wine producers in the land, "You are to supply this young man for a week with the best wine. He should not want. If he requests wine, he should more receive."

"Thank you chief for your kindness." Saye said.

Next, came Nyahn, the Chief asked him, "What it is you desire?"

He said, "Oh Great Chief, I have never tasted such decent cooking in all my life. If it pleases you, could I have as much food as I had yesterday?"

Again, the chief thought this was odd. Food was the least of the things he had expected anyone to ask for. In his land, his people were great cooks, everyone knew that but food was plentiful so the women had plenty time to master their skills. The chief was beginning to think that he erred by allowing these men to give away so much for so little.

As much as he wanted to reconsider, he could not for this was the custom, so he had to obey. He ordered his head wife, "You are to make sure this man gets all the food he can eat. Let him not ever complain about hunger. For a week, make his feeding your priority." Nyahn thanked the chief and left with the head wife to begin eating.

The chief then asked Paye what it was he desired. "Chief, I have seen no finer weaving of cotton or any other fabric than those of your chiefdom. If you so desire, please let me have as much clothes as possible?"

"Just clothes?" the chief asked.

"Yes just that," Paye replied. He was well built like his brothers and handsome, but he had a plan.

The chief thought to himself, "What are these boys thinking?" He finally had to admit that he was mistaken. None of these requests made much sense to him, but as they say, one takes for granted that which one gets so plentiful or so easily. To the chief, their requests were foolish but to these men, they had each requested little things that mattered the most to them.

Thus it was, for one week each had all they desired. The eldest was drunk for most of the week and barely knew what was going on around him. He had become a nuisance. The elder, consumed more food and still had more, his stomach began running after a few days and the food was no longer appealing. The people attending to him were fed up with the mess he made. The youngest, surprisingly seemed to be doing well. Every available maiden in the land and even some fully attached ones sought after him. His looks made him the talk of town. Many of the wealthy families had invited him over for meals. Some sought to lure him into marrying their daughters, others his wealth, for certainly a man who could afford this much had to be wealthy they believed.

Despite this, Paye did not rush to commit to anyone. He had a plan. He decided to choose one special maiden. On the very first day they entered the town, he saw a most beautiful maiden at the chief's palace but only briefly. Later that night, he inquired about her and they told him she was the chief's favorite daughter and talking to her could land him in the gravest danger if the chief was displease. Thus, he remained quiet about his desire and plotted.

When he got his clothes, he made sure to package some of the finest ones. He then presented them to the guards watching over the princess. They refused at first, but when they saw the value of the cloth, he offered in exchange for delivering the items, they agreed. They told him that if caught, they would deny any involvement. They warned him that he risked death if the princess raises any alarm. He agreed and promised to leave them out of any trouble that might arise. He went in to see the princess. He was certain that the looks from the young maiden meant something. Thus, he took the risk to move closer. If it worked he would enjoy his happiness at least for another week, if not he was dead.

The maiden was shocked to see him, yet he was glad. "What are you doing here? How did you get in here?"

"Calm down, stop raising your voice," he hushed her. "No one is going fine out. I have it all under control." He assured her that all was well and the guards would say nothing.

"Are you sure?" she whispered, "The guards are out there somewhere, they could come in and this would be trouble. She was skeptical since no one ever came in here after she retired to bed, then she thought, "If he was here then he must have figured a way she thought. Furthermore, it was good to have a decent company. His good looks was all the better for him."

"It is alright. No one is coming in here. I took care of them."

"Sit down and tell me about you and the place you come from." She instructed. They talked for hours until the early morning when he had to leave.

They carried out this charade for a few days before it turned into a love affair.

When the week was over, the chief summoned his guards to bring forth the three brothers. Saye was drunk and incoherent as usual. He did not even comprehend what was going on. Nyahn had the most upset stomach in his entire life; he was puking and running all over the place. However, when the guards went to get Paye, they could not find him.

They conducted a thorough search of the palace and they still did not find him. Just when the chief began to realize that he had been tricked, his guards informed him that his daughter was missing. He immediately ordered the land searched and offered a huge reward for anyone who would find his daughter.

He had the guards keeping watch over her jailed. Upon questioning, he learned that Paye had visited her. He was furious. At first he thought Paye kidnapped his daughter, but as they searched, he realized that the two eloped.

She had packed enough of his gold an Paye had taken enough expensive cloths along with them. They traveled far into a distant land. They knew that the chief would kill him if they were found. She loved him so much and feared losing him. She also knew her father would not spare him for this act, so their only recourse was to go far away from his land.

They traveled far, far away and eventually ran out of food. They were deep in the forest and at the point of starvation when they met a beautiful maiden, she had bundles of rice and bush meat. She was alone and was traveling with all this food. "Oh maiden, give us rice to eat," pleaded Paye. "We have gold and will exchange some for food."

She looked at him and when she realized how handsome he was, she replied, "I don't want your gold. Instead, I will give you all the food you need if you take me as your wife. I am alone and rather have a strong and handsome man like you as my husband than to have riches."

He wanted to refuse but he knew that they would starve to death. He took his wife aside and said, "Look sweetheart, we need this food. You know that don't you?"

"Yes I do, but marrying a complete stranger for food is not a good idea. I mean you do not even know if she is a witch or something else. How can you agree to this crazy proposal?" his wife responded.

"I know it is a big risk, but what other choice do we have? We can't go on without food. I will not watch you die of hunger when I can do something about it. If she is bad, I will divorce her. After all, I didn't pay any dowry for her. Right now, we need to live; we will cross that bridge if we have to. Please just bear it."

His wife also did not like the idea, but figured they had very little choice, it was either that or they would die. She insisted and was angry he would even consider the idea, but he went over to the stranger and said, "I accept your proposal."

"Good," the maiden replied. "Then it is settled." She was true to her word. She prepared a delicious meal; they all sat and ate like never before. After that, the maiden prepared a place to sleep and that night she and Paye slept together to honor the bond of marriage. Paye's wife was so mad and in pain but had no choice. The next day, the three began their journey. They traveled for so many days and eventually realized they were lost in the forest. They feared wild animals might attack them anytime. Several times already, they had nearly killed. When Paye and his wives thought they could take it no longer, they saw another pretty maiden.

"Thank goodness!" Paye exclaimed. "We have been going in circles in this forest. Several animals have tried killing us. It is good to finally see someone who can help us find our way out of this forsaken place. Do you know the way to the next town?"

"Yes I do," the maiden replied

"Could you please help show us the right way?"

"Sure," the maiden replied.

"Thank you so much. We are so grateful your help. How could we ever repay you for this kindness?" Paye muttered.

She paused, saying, "Now that you mention, there is actually one way to repay me."

"How? In what way? Name it?" Paye excitedly asked.

"You could take me as your wife." She said.

The princess did not believe she heard correctly. "What did you say?" she asked.

"I said he should take me as his wife," replied the maiden.

"You are joking right?" jumped in the second wife.

"No I am not, in fact, the only way I will take you to the next town is if he marries me." The maiden insisted.

Paye was shocked, the princess was furious and the second wife was raging. "You can't marry her, no way. I won't allow it."

"You won't allow what? Is that not the same thing you did? Now that someone else is doing it, you are angry." Paye said.

The princess walked away. Paye was going after her, when the maiden said, "I guess I will just go on my way then." She headed in the opposite direction.

The second wife stood there a moment, then ran after Paye. "Look, we must follow the maiden; she has gone in the opposite direction. If we are quick, we could catch her."

They spent some time convincing the princess. When she agreed, they took the trail, but the maiden was nowhere in sight. They wandered about for nearly a day, their feet were sored, their bodies ached and they had so little energy.

"I think we should rest here," said Paye. "She has gone. We were too late."

"This is your fault," shouted the second wife. "We had the chance to leave this forest and the animals here, but you are so selfish, you turned it down. Now we will all die here."

"I rather die than share my husband with strangers. Where do you know the woman from that you will allow him to marry here? You stole this man, so you don't care, as for me, I suffered to get him and to see him taken by others who do not love him is not easy."

"You talk about love as a child would. What good is your love for him, if we all die horrible deaths in this forest?" you better wise up and think about the future. We will die here if we do not find the next village soon." The second wife said, hissing her teeth as she walked away.

Paye was too tired to do anything. He just sat here and tried to sleep.

As night was falling, they sensed several animals hovering around where they were resting.

Just then, there was some scuffle up ahead, some animals were fighting. They hurriedly gathered their things and fled. When they felt a safe distance and was about to rest, they glimpsed a light moving in the trees. They rushed to its source, behold, the maiden stood next to a tree holding a lantern.

"Oh, you three again; have you considered my offer?" she asked, looking directly at Paye.

"Yes I have, I will respond in just a minute," replied Paye.

The Princess was still furious; she refused to talk to them. Paye and the second wife pleaded with her to see reason. Even the second wife was jealous and did not want him to accept the woman's proposal, but Paye had no choice.

Eventually, he agreed and the maiden led them to the next town the following day after she and Paye had honored their marriage that night. By morning, almost none of the women were talking to each other. None of them was happy with Paye as well except the new wife. She seemed to be getting the most attention from her new husband.

Thus, when they entered the new town, Paye had three wives. They presented themselves to the new chief. They treated them in a bad manner. Then the Chief told them to get some rest and return tomorrow. That night, some of the attendants informed them that they had erred by coming to this town. The chief did not like strangers at all and he would ensure that they all die tomorrow or soon afterwards. This news was saddening to them, but what could they do? They were already here and there was no escaping it.

The next morning, the chief summoned them, he informed them, "I have a test for you to take, if you pass it, then I know you came in true peace, but if you fail, then you all would surely die. Do you understand this?"

"Yes chief," Paye replied.

The Chief continued, "The test is this. I have a hundred boxes of gold; you must choose which one of the boxes I owned in my youth."

"What!" The wives thought, more out of shock than anything else. "How did the chief expect Paye to know the answer?" Paye's wives were dismayed for they feared he would miss the answer and they would all die.

"Are you ready to answer or do you need time? Remember, you only have three trials." The chief cautioned. He sat back and relaxed. He did not expect Paye to guess correctly, so he had on a smirk.

Paye pondered for a while and said, "I think the box you owned in your youth is the one over there," Paye pointed to the last box on the left.

"No, that is not the box," the chief replied.

Paye surveyed all the boxes again, and then said, "That box," indicating the middle box.

"I am sorry, you are wrong," said the chief.

By this time, his wives were all certain they were all dead. The boxes were too many and all looked alike. There was no way he could get it right with just one chance left.

Finally, Paye, walked around the boxed and took a little while longer before he spoke. "The box you own when you were young is..."

"Please get it right," the princess whispered.

The second wife could barely breathe, the court was spacious but she was suffocating. Everyone held his or her breath, waiting to see what would happen.

"This one," Paye held the eighth box from the right.

Dead silence filled the room, the new maiden doubled over, refusing to lift her head, "We are dead, she thought."

The chief, after what seemed like forever, slowly nodded, indicating that Paye was correct. He could not form words. The shock of Paye's answer was hard to miss.

The chief took a long time to respond. Finally, he cleared his throat and said, "You have guessed right, and as such, you are entitled to choose one thing you value or up to half of my kingdom as your reward."

Paye looked back at his wives, all of whom were overjoyed. Turned in the direction of the court and said, "I have made by choice," Paye said. "I wish the hand of your daughter."

Two of his wives fainted. The other remained in shock. The chief stood in disbelief. He wasn't please at all but he had to honor rules. He could not refuse the request, so he said, "Very well son, you shall have her."

What they did not know was, that night, Paye afraid of failing the test, gave the guards protecting the chief's daughter, some of the finest linen to allow him to meet her. When he did, he offered her his finest gifts of cloths. Dazzled by this handsome young man, who was obviously wealthy enough to give her that much fine cloth, she agreed to be his wife, in exchange for her father's secrets. This time Paye did not consult his wives. He knew that there was no way they would accept this, moreover, it was a matter of life and death, so he did what he believed he had to in order to get the answer to the question.

By the time his wives woke up, the chatter in the court had reduced considerably. The chief was talking. He told Paye, "There is one rule we price in this chiefdom. We do not allow a man to have many wives. Therefore, you must select one of these women to be your wife and with whom you shall have your children. Whichever choice you make, we will accept."

One woman had abandoned her family for love.

The other had saved him from starvation.

Another had saved him from dying in the forest at the hands of wild animals.

Yet another had saved him from having his head removed by giving him the correct answer.

Which one shall Paye choose to bear his children and live with forever?

CHAPTER XI

The Monkey and the Leopard

Mr. Monkey and Mr. Leopard were once friends, in fact they were even good friends at that time. One day, and little quarrel turned a bit heated. Over time, pride and ego made things bad. From then onward, things went further south and they became the worse enemies in the forest. The leopards delighted in eating monkeys. They were forever devising schemes to catch and feed on monkeys. No one knew the root of the problem anymore. All they did was follow the tradition of enmity between the two species.

It so happened that one day Mr. Leopard lay in cool place resting and thinking. He knew he was not getting any younger and the hunt was proving more difficult. The chasing and climbing were harder than before. In order to survive, he had to find a way to get food constantly. After hours of thinking, he decided to make friends with Mr. Monkey. The leopard figured he could trick him into a friendship and when the monkey's guards were down, he could kill him.

He went to a huge tree where he knew Mr. Monkey frequented and waited. When the Monkey Chief arrived, he was alarmed. He instructed his wives to hide along with the children. He then climbed to the highest and lightest tree branch to keep an eye on leopard.

The wives of Mr. Monkey were having hard time controlling the children who had taken to throwing at Mr. Leopard rotten fruits, branches and whatever else they could lay their hands on. They added insults to the pelting. Their fathers did not really mind and showed little interests in stopping them. The mothers were scared in case one fell down by mistake.

However, the leopard stayed there and waited for a monkey to come close enough within his reach. Eventually, Mr. Monkey came along as if to say, "I am watching you old guy."

Mr. Leopard greeted him, he said, "Look, we have not done ourselves any good with this enmity. I think it is time we place it behind us. I am here to offer my friendship." He explained, I think we should stop. We have fought for so long, even our children have gotten involved, and it was time we stopped and live in peace. I am serous about this; I don't wish it to go on anymore."

Mr. Monkey was skeptical and he did not hide it. "Really? Why the sudden change of heart? Are you tired with monkey meat? Just tell me why?"

The leopard was silent, and then finally he said, "Since my youth, I have sought and killed monkeys and frankly I don't see the reason to continue especially now that I am old and about to die, I seek only peace. I do not want to leave behind such a bad name."

The monkey still not convinced said, "Okay, we will see how true you are to your words."

"Oh, I am. In fact, Mr. Monkey to show you that I am, I brought you and your wives some fruits to seal this pact."

The monkey said, "Just leave the offerings under the tree and step back a safe distance." He did so and the monkey snatched up what he could and was back up the three before the leopard had the chance to do anything. To his surprise, Mr. Leopard did not move an inch. He continued snatching until he had all the items up safely. In all that time, the leopard did not move a muscle.

Afterwards, he came a bit lower and talked with his new guest. Mr. Leopard asked him, "Don't you want to live in peace?"

"Of course I do," the monkey explained. "So does the other monkeys. I do not want to have to look over my shoulders all the time. I do not want to stop my children from freely playing in fear of an attack. However, the reality is you give us no other option but to do so."

The talk lasted long. Eventually, Mr. Leopard requested something. "How do you manage to swing so freely and fast? I wish to learn the swinging magic. Could you teach me? I mean you are the best swingers I know."

"Your words are sweet," the Monkey Chief agreed, "but your teeth, though old and yellow, are still sharp. You can't expect us to just take this proposal without discussion. This matter must be considered by our entire council, so call again tomorrow and we will tell you our decision."

"Sure," said the leopard. "I don't expect you to trust me just like that. So, take your time and discuss it. In the end, you will see that I mean real peace."

The next morning, before Mr. Leopard came to meet them, the Monkey Chief placed a basket beneath the huge tree and waited. When the Leopard cane he said, "Oh Mr. Leopard, we have considered your proposal. It seems good for all of us, but you can understand how hard it is for us to trust you. We have decided to test your honor. Do you see the baskets under the tree? Take it to your house, but do not open it. Don't sniff it. Do nothing to it, but return it tomorrow as it was given to you."

Mr. Leopard needed to win the hearts of the monkeys so he tried his best to ignore his cravings. He focused on the overall aim of his plan. He lifted the basket and it felt empty. He thought, "What a fool. What is an empty basket going to do to me?" He smiled to himself as he carried the basket. He had expected a tough challenge from the Monkey Chief.

He thought they would even have asked him to eat with them or be close to them and test his ability to restrain himself from eating one person. Now that would have been a real test. He knew how difficult it was to stop his desire to jump on one of those monkeys.

Instead, he got this foolish exercise. He went home. He dropped the basket in a corner and asked, "Where is my meal?"

"Which meal?" When last did you bring home food?" she asked.

"Are you telling me there is nothing in this house to eat? What about the meat I brought the other day?" he inquired.

She said, "Are you listening to yourself? The other day you say. What do you think we have been eating? There is very little left. Whatever you are planning should work out fast or we would starve."

He exhaled and hissed. "This woman. When will she learn to manage? Does she not know I am old and can't hunt as before?" he thought to himself.

When his wife enquired, "How about your visit to the monkeys, how did it go?"

He laughed loudly. "Those monkeys are fools," he told her. "Do you know what the chief asked me to do? He asked me to bring this basket home and return it tomorrow without looking into it or sniffing or opening it.

The wife seemed puzzled. "Is something inside?" she asked.

He shook his head. "I did not look. Anyway, I don't think so; it is too light to hold anything.

She thought for a moment and said, "Maybe it is a trick. Maybe there is something inside; a small monkey perhaps?"

"That is outrageous woman!" he bellowed. "I took the thing from the tree to here and it weighs nothing," he explained.

"Then why do you think they gave you all those warnings?" the wife asked.

He shrugged and said, "Because they are foolish I suppose." His wife tried convincing him to look in the box, just to be sure or to at least sniff it, but he refused. He reminded her that he was not going to break the promise. He had to convince the monkeys that he was trust-worthy. This was the only way to ensure their survival in their old age. He scorned his wife for being shortsighted and not caring enough for him. Here she was forcing him to break the deal and forgetting that he was old and would not be able to hunt much longer. The woman said nothing more. She just quietly listened.

He told her of his plan. "I intend to win the trust of the monkeys. When I do, I would sneak into their homes when they sleep and kill a few. Their guards would be down and I wouldn't leave a trace. Besides, we would be friends then so they would not suspect him. This is how we will get our regular meals for the rest of our lives. I think the plan was simple and brilliant. What do you think?" he asked his wife.

His wife did not see things that way. "I am not sure about this. I figure they would suspect you first for any missing monkey. She knew that nothing was simple with the Monkeys. They were far too smart for that. She tried telling her husband but he would not listen. Thus, they slept without opening the basket.

The next day, Leopard returned to the tree with the basket. The Monkey Chief was relieved seeing the basket but he was still scared, for he did not trust the leopard. Maybe he had eaten his son and returned the basket in an attempt to catch a few more for his meal. He cautiously approached the basket after the Leopard had stepped back a safe distance. He took it up the tree and gathered the council. Upon inspection, he confirmed that it was unopened.

What the leopard did not know was that the monkey had outsmarted him this was no ordinary basket. The basket was a strong one made of cane and bamboo and tied with ropes. The Monkey Chief had placed his thinnest son inside. He securely fastened him deep inside the basket and covered him up.

The little monkey heard all the discussions of Mr. and Mrs. Leopard. He then explained the plans of Mr. Leopard to the council. The Monkey Chief, who had suspected something odd about the Leopard's request, got his confirmation.

He returned to the leopard and said, "I have good news for you. You have passed the test. It was now time to teach him our swinging magic, but first, I have to convince the others that you are serious to learn. Personally, I am convinced but some of the others have concerns and need to be reassured. They were worried over how you planned to sustain your diet now that you are off monkey meat. They wanted a demonstration.

"Sure, whatever it is," said Mr. Leopard.

Monkey tossed a banana and some fruits over at Mr. Leopard. He chewed the banana with its peel on it because he did not know how to remove it. He did the same with the other fruits. This was disgusting to him but he pretended to be fine as he swallowed. After this display, the Monkey Chief announced to all that Mr. Leopard had proved his commitment to peace so they should welcome him and consider him a friend from now onwards.

He called for a huge celebration. Then the strongest males came down along with a few wise and fast females. They had not wanted to raise the leopard's suspicion. In the midst of the merry making, when they were all relaxed and full of palm wine, they offered to show their new friend the secret to their swinging. The monkeys carried him up a tree branch and they tied his tail to it. When they were assured that he was securely tied up, they all came down and began pelting him with sticks, fruits, stones and any other object.

He was shocked, for he had believed his plan had worked. For two days, the monkeys stoned him almost to death. The more they did, the angrier he got. He tried to free himself but couldn't. The mixture of wine and being tied up tightly made it impossible. His wife came to his rescue after he failed to return the day before. Thus, it is today whenever a leopard is angry it swings it tails as he did that day when trying to free himself from the monkeys.

CHAPTER XII

Musa the Trapper

Once, long ago, there lived a very poor man named Musa. He had no family and almost no friends. He was so poor he had to beg for food from time to time. At other times, he would offer his service as a laborer on the farms of others. In fact, he even traveled to surrounding villages and towns looking for work. He would brush on farms or take bags of fruits or other foodstuffs to the markets for his bosses. There was just nothing too small for him to do.

It so happened that one day, on one of his trips to the next big market, he felt dizzy and weary. At first, he thought it was because of the weight of the cassava bag he was carrying. However, it persisted and it was so overpowering that Musa could bear it no longer. He found the nearest shaded area and he sat to rest beneath the biggest tree. It was not long after, then he was *gone*.

Later, Musa approached the gates of the most beautiful city he had ever seen. He was so dazzle by the clean streets, the nicely whitewashed houses, the neatly placed thatch roofs on the homes and everything seemed big, larger than anything he had ever seen. As he was admiring these sights, he saw something that would change his life forever.

Standing in the back of a nicely built village house was the most beautiful maiden Musa had ever laid his eyes on. He stopped in his tracks and unknowingly to him, his jaws dropped open. He stood staring for what seemed like eternity. Slowly, she turned around as if sensing the stare and she gave Musa the warmest and prettiest smile of his life. His heart almost stopped beating when she waved him over.

Musa's legs could not respond to the command coming from his mind. It was as if he was rooted in the spot. Eventually, he mustered the strength to move his legs. He barely dragged them along. When he reached her, she asked, "What is your name?"

"Musa," he whispered.

"Nice to meet you, she said as she handed him a stool to sit. "My name is Varbah and I live in this house with my mother. Let me prepare something for you. What do you wish to eat?" she asked him.

He could not find his voice, so he shook his head as if to say "Nothing."

"You must be hungry, also as a stranger in town, I insist that you have some food and take some water along when you leave, this is our custom. Musa couldn't refuse even if he wished it. Therefore, he simply nodded his head for fear that his voice might fail him.

She returned in no time and handed him a calabash of cold water. Although Musa was thirsty, he hardly touched the water. He kept staring and stealing glances at Varbah, as she prepared something for him to eat. Although, it was customary in this city to serve strangers water and some food, Varbah found herself liking this guy more than she cared to admit the more they talked. He was not like the rest of the young men in the village. He was just different. She could not tell what it was about him but she sensed something unique about him.

After Musa had eaten and he was full to capacity, he asked "Varbah could you please show me the way to the chief's court?"

"Sure, I will take you there." She really wanted to know more about Musa. They talked along the way and in no time found that they had so many things in common. Varbah was a great dancer and Musa could sing. She plaited her natural long wooly hair in corned roles. She had open teeth and full lips. She had nicely curved hips shaped in the right proportion. She also had big tumba.

Over the next few days, Musa and Varbah were inseparable. They had fallen in love at first sight and were taking advantage of each moment they could get. Folks all over town would see these two lovebirds. They found every excuse to be together. They enjoyed each other's company and Varbah showed Musa his way around the city.

Suddenly, Musa was facing a very serious problem. He loved Varbah very much and wanted to marry her. He had said as much to her. The hitch to this plan was he had no money to purchase the necessary gifts for her mother or the ceremony. Since begging brought no wealth, he realized that he had to find a way to get Varbah all the things she needed to get married.

Musa knew of a way to solve his predicament. He was hardworking and he knew that animals abounded outside the city walls. He decided to be a trapper. This way he will secure both food for himself and skins for trade. He planned on hunting and selling his game to provide for Varbah and save for his wedding.

Musa began his new profession with the kind of zeal only love can provide. He made fifty traps and set them all over a particular part of the forest. It was hard work but he was sure that it was worth it. He admired his work after he was done. Musa went home and told Varbah the good news. They were both excited. They made a decision to tell Varbah's mother about their planned marriage.

The mother accepted temporarily under two conditions. One, Varbah must be accepted into the prestigious Sande Society. Two, Musa must prove that he is capable of taking good care of her daughter. Seeing that her father had died, this was paramount to the final agreement. She gave Musa up to the end of the acceptance ceremony. If he succeeded in proving himself capable of being a great husband to Varbah, then she was all his. If not, she would be married off to another suitor.

This seemed reasonable to Musa. First, he had some time to prove himself. Secondly, he had prepared enough traps that would give him plenty game from which he could sell the skin and the other parts of the animal to pay for his bride. Musa and Varbah were so optimistic about things. They kept on planning their life together. Where they would live, how they would build their house and what they would buy to place inside the house from the game money.

It was with high hopes that Musa went into the forest the next day to check on his traps. He had not finished his rounds when he saw a huge doe stuck in one of his traps. Musa leapt for joy at this sight. He rushed to the trap and started to untie the doe when he heard a loud, frightening voice saying, "Give me the doe."

Musa looked around partly out of fear and bewilderment. He saw no one or nothing else except a huge black rock near the trap.

Making no sense out of this, he began to remove the trap only to hear the same voice but this time louder than before saying, "Give me the doe. I am the Spirit of the black Rock. You must place any animal in your trap on the top of my head or I will rise and swallow you! Just place the doe on my head and leave now!" Musa was astonished to hear the rock speak, moreover for it to threaten him. Being fearful of the threat, he placed his animal on the top of its head.

Almost as quickly, as Musa placed it there, the animal disappeared into the rock. It just vanished like that; in a big swoosh! This scared Musa out of his pants. "Not only can the rock talk," he thought, "it can also make things disappear." Musa wanted nothing more than to be as far away as he could, from this rock spirit. He dropped his bag and took off in a way he had never run before.

Musa ran at full speed and when he thought he was at a safe distance from the Spirit Rock, he stopped to catch his breath. He was panting so hard that the sound of his heart was all he could hear in the forest. He debated over going home or staying in the forest in search of another spot to lay his traps. He finally made up his mind to relocate. He loved Varbah too much to give up on her.

He scouted the forest and found just the right place for game. He shifted his traps to that general area. He set twice as many traps as before. All the while, he was checking and jumpy at any noise. He feared he might not have gotten far enough away from the Rock Spirit. He soon realized that it was just his fear that was trying to have better of him. Despite this, Musa carried on setting his traps in the best locations.

In the evening, after he had set all his traps, he went home. He was afraid to tell his beloved Varbah about what had happened. Seeing that it was his first day, his mother-in-law did not bother him. When Varbah came to see him, he talked about how he had set his traps in the best places and soon they would be full of game. He assured her that there was no better place, in the forest, than where he had laid his traps. This was good news and she seemed happy.

Early the next morning, he set of for the forest. This time he made sure to check that no one followed him. When he had satisfied himself, he began checking on his traps. Soon enough it paid off. Musa saw locked in his trap and full-grown lion. His heart leapt for joy. This was really a good catch. He imagined how much he could make from the meat alone and how much food he could provide his maiden and his mother in law. Musa's adrenaline was pumping faster now. He went to the trap quickly and started untying the lion.

Just when he was done, he heard the familiar voice, "Give me your game."

"Oh no way," Musa thought to himself. He could not believe his ears. Had he not known better, he would have thought his mind was playing tricks on him. He raised his head and behold there lay the Black Rock. The very Spirit Rock he thought he had avoided had moved to this part of the forest and again demanded the animal in his trap. He hesitated for the briefest of moments but decided to give the lion to the Spirit Rock. Again, as soon as Musa placed the animal on top of the rock it disappeared. He proceeded to his next trap and the rock followed him to it and demanded the catch. Musa had thought that by giving the rock the first animal it would have been satisfied but that was not going to happen he realized.

After the Rock had taken the last of the animals from Musa's trap, it left. Certain he was alone; he decided to scout a more distant part of the forest. This time he walked for almost the whole day. He was convinced that game was plentiful in this forest and all he had to do was avoid the parts that the Spirit Rock visited. Musa walked until his legs were sore and almost swollen. He was certain that the Rock had not followed him this far. It could not possibly have.

Whilst laying his traps, Musa worked with more anger and hatred than fear. He placed thrice as many traps and worked until darkness fell on the forest. He was determined to take home something for his Varbah and her mother. He wanted to impress her early on so she would have no reason to want to entertain another proposal for her daughter. He knew Varbah loved him and was counting on him to win her mother's heart. It was all up to him now.

When Musa got home that day, he was so tired that he could hardly walk, let alone eat the food his mother-in-law had prepared for him. She asked after his trapping business and he gave her the good news.

When Varbah returned, she also got the optimism of the first day.

On day three, Musa was determined to get to his traps before the Rock did. He left home before dawn and was well into the forest before anyone had gotten up. He planned to check around carefully before getting to any of his traps. He was taking no chances today. He had to outsmart the Spirit or the whole Musa and Varbah love affair would be history. Just before he reached the first trap, he heard a strange sound. It took him a moment to place it and then it hit him! It was an elephant. He had landed gold. His trap had given him an elephant. It was not yet dead which means he could carry fresh meat to his in-laws and sell the rest to the big market.

Musa wasted no time in putting the elephant down. He removed the most valuable parts. He was so happy he had finally out weighted the Spirit Rock. He was about to leave the trap and call others to help him when the Spirit Rock appeared out of nowhere demanding the elephant. "No way, over my dead body," Musa thought. "This time I intended to put up a fight. I am not going to lose my meat just like that. No way is this evil act going to happen today," he continued his thought.

It was as if the Rock could read his mind. It told him, "Musa, do not try anything foolish. Have you forgotten that I can swallow you up before you can even act? I am mighty and powerful, I can devour you in no time." Although he was still resolved to hold on to his meat, the images of the Rock swallowing the other animals flashed and Musa reluctantly agreed.

He swore at the Rock and made all kinds of threats, but these he knew were for nothing. If anything, they served only to appease him a little for his losses. He was so furious he began to shake as if he was possessed.

After the Rock had devoured the elephant, it stopped talking. Musa stood there for a long time, a million thoughts running through his mind, all of them involved how he could get rid of the Spirit Rock. He just did not know of any way to this.

Finally he went back home, but his mother-in-law was not so understanding. She asked him, "What is going on? I really want to know why you have gotten no game so far. Do I need to remind you that time is drawing closer and you have not caught a single animal? When will you live up to your end of the arrangement? If you are sure you still want to marry my daughter, you had better start acting fast."

Varbah walked in and heard her mother say these things to him and it saddened her. When her mother left, she tried to console Musa. This was not helping at all, as he was still upset. Finally, he decided to tell her the truth. Upon hearing this, she tried hard to stay calm. She even suggested he seeks the Chief Spiritualist's advice on ways of appeasing this Rock Spirit. He agreed to do that. They went there, but this too did not work out as the spiritualist told him that there was little he could do about it. He just had to wait until the rock was satisfied or until it found another person from whom to gather meals.

For many days, this went on; and it seemed that no matter where he put his traps, the Rock Spirit was sure to follow. In the end, Musa would have no animals to take home. This would warrant more insults from Varbah's mother. The closer the ceremony drew the angrier Varbah's mother became. She seemed to be increasing the level of insult and her attitude to Musa was nastier by the day.

In fact, one time she told her daughter to leave Musa for he was useless. He could not take care of a woman. This she said in the presence of Musa. At another time, she was so angry she exclaimed, "Oh worthless hunter! Do you hunt animals, or do they haunt you? You ask to wed my daughter, yet you bring no gifts. You wish to have her as your wife, yet you cannot feed yourself, I will not have my daughter marry such a poor and worthless fool."

"Mother please stop saying such horrible things." This hurt Varbah so badly. She tried her best to make peace between her mother and Musa but her mother would not relent. Many days she cried and feared that her mother, who had come to using her threat of denying Musa Varbah's hand daily, would actually carry out this threat. She and Musa tried all they could but things remained the same on the mother's end.

Meanwhile, Musa's bad luck continued. He and Varbah grieved at this, for they loved each other dearly. The time had just about finished and they knew that her mother would make good on her promise. In fact, she had not fail to inform Musa each time a new suitor made his intention known to her. Each time she received a gift or present from a viable suitor, for Varbah's hand, she flaunted it in Musa's face. Things rapidly deteriorated. All this while, Musa put in more effort on his trapping. He had exhausted every viable spot in the forest. Each time the results were the same and without knowing it, time was upon them.

On the evening before the ceremonies of the Sande Society, Musa went once more into the forest, though his heart was heavy inside him. His traps were empty. He wasn't surprised since he had shared all the animals he caught in the forest. He had been obliged to give each of them to the Spirit of the Black Rock. He checked the other ones, the same results. Finally, he cried out at the Spirit of the Black Rock, "What have I done to you that you hate me so much?" He demanded. "Answer me!" He was desperate now and almost did care at all. He did not even fear the Rock Spirit. He was just livid and frustrated that all his best efforts had gone in vain.

He entertained no illusion of bringing back any meat this day. In fact, he went to the forest in part to get away from the incessant nagging of his mother-in-law and to give the spirit a piece of his mind. In despair he sat down on the rock himself, hoping the spirit might devour him too. Nothing happened. He got up and sat down harder on the top of the Rock, still nothing happened. He remained there with his hands under his cheeks in a defeated pose. It seemed like forever still nothing happened.

Suddenly, the black rock said to him, "Oh hunter, for a month and more you have given me every animal you caught, and now I shall reward you for your labors. Beat me seven times with your stick." Musa did not have time for any of the Rock Spirit's tricks. He did not know what new ploy it was up to now but he did not intend to find out. As he sat there determined not to play into the Rock's hand, he heard that so familiar voice, "Oh hunter hit me with your stick seven times."

He paused for a while, and then he thought, "What was there to lose after all?" He got up slowly from the rock, picked up his stick then dropped it after pausing. He walked a few paces away into the forest and returned with the biggest stick that he could lay his hands on. Musa approached the rock and images of his meat vanishing on top of that Rock flooded his mind. He raised that stick way above his head. He was not focusing clearly. He brought it down with all his might. He beat the Rock once and the stick broke. He picked it up again and repeatedly knocked the rock. He pounded it as if it was the last thing he would do in this life.

He was out of breath when he stopped. The stick was shattered and its splinters lay all around him on the floor. He felt a whole lot relieved and wanted to do more. His face brightened at the thought of having to get back at the Rock Spirit. He was savoring his small revenge so much that he failed to notice the area immediately around the Rock. When he finally got hold of himself, his eyes fell on them. For a moment, he thought he was dreaming. He knocked his head with his hand just to be sure, that he was actually seeing it.

On the floor, all around the Black Rock lay huge stone size pieces of gold. In all, one piece for each strike Musa had given the Rock. They were so large that he could barely fit one in his hand let alone two of them. Musa fainted. After a while, he came through, composed himself and hauled all the gold to a secure location very close to the village. This process took the whole night and most of the early morning. He hid them well, taking only a few pieces with him.

Musa went into the first big city along the route to his village and traded the gold. The gold pieces were so valuable that several goldsmiths had to join their resources together just to get the fair value of the gold he brought.

Musa then went on a buying spree. He got the finest dresses and jewelry money could buy. He sent word out that he sought to hire the best dancing crew in the whole country. He added the best singers to this group and got the fastest runners to take his goods to his village. He had well-built men take him around in a hammock as if he was royalty. He changed into the most expensive clothes he could find and got himself a nice haircut. By the time he was done, no one who knew him could recognize him.

His hired hands carried him to his town. Along the way, he gave chiefs presents and their wives gifts.

In no time, the word spread that a powerful prince was travelling through the kingdom and disposing gifts indiscriminately. At each palace, when asked where he was going, Musa told the same story. He was heading for the Sande Society's graduation ceremony. He wanted to marry the fairest maiden that was graduating from that school today.

This response always seemed to bring up interest from his hosts. They all wanted to see who this beautiful maiden was. Many wished that their daughters were the lucky maiden. Some even offered to give him any maiden he liked in their chiefdom. This was only a ploy to get some more of his riches and Musa knew it very well. He had no plans to miss out on his Varbah. They had suffered together, now was the time for her to enjoy along with him.

By the time Musa reached his village, the place was crowded. The ceremonies were just beginning. The maidens had paraded the town once and their family and loved ones were cheering them on. Varbah appeared happy, but deep down, she was sad that she had not seen Musa. Her mother on the other hand, was so hyperactive. She was imagining the presents and gifts that the suitors would offer today when they see how beautiful her Varbah was. She had even forgotten about Musa. Her mind was on finding the best suitor for her daughter and preferably one that was man enough to take good care of her.

The news that an extremely handsome and wealthy prince, from a distant land, was on his way in search for a maiden had taken the town by storm.

Every mother or father with a daughter of marriageable age was hoping it would be his or her lucky day. The dancers and musicians that Musa hired had reached the village and were performing to their best. All the surrounding towns had come to see them perform. These performers were without a doubt the best in the whole chiefdom and no one wanted to miss this chance. They poured in until there was almost no space in town for the graduates to parade.

Musa entered the town like a king. The fanfare and merry making was as no one had seen in a while. He ordered some of his hired helps to secretly decorate and stand guard at Varbah's house. She and her mother had no way of knowing this as they were caught, like many others, in the other part of the town. They gave him a prime seat at the graduation ceremony. He had already spoiled the king and his wives with presents.

As all the special guests sat and watched the young maidens parading around in their nice attires and braided hair, Musa kept fixing his eyes on Varbah but he tried not to let her see him. The king had asked him several times that he was free to select any one he liked, but Musa had nodded kindly and said he would consider that kind offer.

All this while, Varbah kept searching the crowd for a glimpse of her darling Musa. She hoped that he would show up and give her the moral support. She did not care about gifts or presents right now. She needed to see him. She finally got close enough to her mother for a brief moment and made the terrible mistake of asking, "Have you seen Musa?"

"What! You foolish girl! Which Musa?" Her mother yelled at her. "That useless boy? Why are you still focusing on him when all these other good suitors are here? I even here there is a wealthy prince here from a distant land and he want to marry someone from the class. So, if you know what is good for you, just do your best to impress him and stop this nonsense about Musa business."

"I just thought he would be here for the ceremony today," she said.

"But do you see him? No. He is not here. For all you know, the worthless man has run away out of shame. Do not worry I have better proposals available regarding the marriage. Things are on the up and I will find the best man for you."

"Okay Mama," she said. Varbah did not feel that way but she didn't say. She was just trying to make her mother happy.

"Yes child, today is your graduation day, so try and enjoy yourself okay?"

"Yes, Mama, I will," she responded.

"Like I said, focus on wooing in the wealthy guests seated nears the king. Most of your friends are doing that and here you are wasting your time on a good for nothing Musa; a man who could not provide for a woman." This angered Varbah but she decided to ignore it. She was still searching the crowd hoping to steal a glance of him. The one place she was not looking was at the king's sitting area and that was her only mistake.

Perhaps if she had looked in that direction carefully or if she was trying hard, like the other maidens to impress the rich prince, she might have, on chance, noticed the stares he was stealing at her. However, the thought did not cross her mind in the least. This suited Musa fine, for it gave him the liberty to look at her without her noticing him doing so.

Eventually, suitors picked each maiden. Varbah's mother received various proposals but she refused hoping for a better one than the previous. She wanted to get the most she could for her daughter. This greediness caused her to miss the better offers available. Thus, Varbah remained the only maiden old enough to get married that had not gotten a suitor. All the best maidens had suitors and yet the prince had chosen none. This was strange in a way. Many had hoped he would pick them but he had not.

Now it seems as if he did not like any of the women in this town and he might just go back as he had come, empty-handed. This was a situation the king was determined not to allow to happen under his rule. This was disgraceful to say the least. He was trying everything he knew to get the prince to select a maiden from his town. He even had all the suitable maidens paraded several times over hoping the prince would change his mind or he had missed something earlier. However, the prince still did not choose any. If the prince left without selecting anyone, it would be most shameful for his village.

They were not happy but not much, they could do about it. They had given their best shots. Furthermore, the other maidens were glad to be selected. The only person that was sad the most was Varbah's mother. Varbah was elated for this meant that maybe her mother would finally give her hand to Musa to avoid the shame. Her greed made her refuse the earlier offers.

The graduation was over and those unpicked maidens, in this case Varbah alone, had to go home, disgracefully, without fanfare.

Just when all had given up hope of the prince taking a maiden from this town, he got up and walked towards Varbah. At first, it looked as if he was leaving since he headed for the direction that leads out of the town. He and his performers went through the town with the crowd in his wake.

At a newly decorated house, he paused. Here he deposited all the things he purchased. They included the richest gowns, jewels, and fine gifts and many others. Attended by dancers and musicians he rode in glory through the gates leading to the house. Her mother and the others marveled among themselves to see the mighty young prince who had come this far for the sake of love.

Varbah's mother was a bit behind in the crowd, she didn't even recognize the house as hers. All those at the back knew was that the royal party had stopped at a house. He entered and found Varbah, seated and her head bowed. She was sad about Musa and angry with her mother for pushing him away.

She did not even want to see what all the noise was about although it was happening right outside her fence. She figured the prince had chosen one of her closest friends both of whom lived right next door.

It wasn't until she heard her name that she stood up to look outside. She was sure she recognized the voice of Musa. She came running outside to see, only to find herself facing the prince who happened to be Musa. She fainted. When she came through, servants were attending her and Musa was smiling down at her. "This is impossible," she thought. "It can't be Musa."

Eventually, he came around to telling her the story. Thus, Musa married his beloved Varbah, and days of feasting followed. Two months had passed since his wedding. Yet people were still feasting at their place. He and his bride lived in a palace with honor and wealth and unaccustomed wealth. He got a house for his mother-in-law as far away from them as possible. He had had enough of her and was not going to let her interfere in his new life. He did all he could to keep her away yet happy.

However, as time passed and Musa learned the power of his wealth grew arrogant, as well as fat. He dealt harshly with his servants. He was rude and at times abusive to them. He mistreated them at the slightest error they made. Varbah was always trying hard to make them feel better. In fact, they loved her very much. Many times, she tried to get him to go soft on them but he would act nice only for a short while.

Then one day, he fell ill with a strange illness. All the diviners in the town came and treated him but nothing seemed to be working. In fact, it seemed as if the more they tried the worse he got. Eventually, they had to send for the most famous diviner in the whole kingdom. When he came, he administered some herbs, which helped Musa a bit. The Great Diviner said that he had to read Musa's palm. After cutting his sands, he said, "A bag of cassava weighs heavily on your spirit. Eat no more cassava, or your spirit's strength will break."

Varbah did not understand the meaning of this but she made sure, Musa ate no more cassava. Soon after, he grew well, but in no time, he began his old ways. He became so haughty that his servants came to hate him more than before. Everyone had given up on him except Varbah. He kept changing servants or they kept leaving him. He did not seem to care for he had enough money to replace them immediately they left his service.

Despite Varbah's best efforts, Musa did not change. She even suggested bringing her mother. "I think Mama should help around with the chores."

"What!" he said. This only infuriated Musa the more. "You are joking right? I will not hear of it. That woman tormented me and you want her to come in my house to do more to me? No way. She is fine right where she is. We provide for her and she has all she needs. I don't need her here creating trouble and making my home unhappy."

"But what you are doing is making this home unhappy. You terrify the servants and make everyone around you unhappy. Just be careful, I don't want any bad happening to you. Try to treat others with respect too. You never used to be this way." Varbah said.

"Oh, so you want me to spend my money hiring people who will just laze around here and not do my work?" he asked.

"I'm not saying that Musa, you know it."

"Well then what do you want me to do with them when they are lazing around and not working? Should I pet them?"

"It's okay," Varbah said. "We should not argue. You always get this way," as he stormed out.

One day, after he had so badly treated a new servant, he sent her to prepare food for him. She was so frightened she did not know what to do. She rushed in the market and got food to prepare for her master. She had no time so she got the first things she saw. She even had the hunter give her the deer meat without taking out the pellets. She could do it when she got home. She fixed the food and took it to her master who wasted no time in gutting it all. Musa had gotten so chubby that one could hardly recognize him.

As soon as he had taken the last spoon, he felt a strange sensation in his belly. He had no time to think what it was that was making him uncomfortable. He screamed for Varbah who rushed out to meet him bent over. Before she could reach him, and in the presence of all the others, there was a loud hollow noise and he completely disappeared. They were all shocked for none had seen such a thing before. Varbah asked the servants what had happened but no one seemed to know. The cooked looked as if she would die. She kept shaking.

Varbah asked her, "What did you prepared?"

As soon as Varbah heard "Cassava," she fainted. No one told her Musa doesn't eat cassava.

Musa woke up underneath the tree deep in the forest. His waistcloth was rotten, pigs had long ago eaten his bagful of cassava, his body was dirty and his hair was the home of insects. He had been rich and lived in a palace with the loveliest of wives and best of life. He could not understand what he was doing here, more so looking horrible as this.

What he did not know was that he had been dreaming and the dream had broken. He had slept for a long time, and since he was a poor and unimportant man, no one came looking for him. As he slept, he dreamed he entered a great city, and there he met a fair maiden called Varbah, the two young people fell in love, and Musa agreed to marry Varbah as soon as she graduated from the Sande Society.

He had returned to poverty and he would remain in poverty, for he had destroyed his fortune with arrogance, and pride. It was as the result of his own doing that was back to this poor life. The Rock Spirit juju could no longer work if Musa got proud and arrogant. It had worked at first because he was humble enough to share his game with the Rock.

CHAPTER XIII

Taywah's Choice

Watta/Taywah was the most beautiful maiden in the land. She was tender, soft spoken and graceful. She was also a good dancer. She passed the Bush School as one of the best students. Every boy in town wished her hand in marriage, so did many men. However, there was a problem. In fact two problems.

First, Taywah was the daughter of the most powerful Paramount Chief. This eliminated most of the young men from the race. Thus, only Paramount Chiefs, Clan Chiefs, princes and great warriors could ask her hand in marriage. Secondly, Taywah's father loved her so much that he promised to allow her to choose her own suitor.

Despite this, she was mean and selfish. She loved herself more than she loved anyone else. Anything she did, served only to benefit her first and maybe others. If that was not possible, she really did not mind.

When she reached the age of marriage, her father made good on his promise that she could select her suitor. He sent word to all ends of his kingdom and even to distant lands way beyond is kingdom. Great warriors, powerful chiefs and handsome heirs came from all over to express interest in the maiden.

However, maiden used the freedom her father allowed her carelessly. She told her father that, "Papa, I want a spotless man; one without a blemish."

"What! Are you sure this is what you want?" the father asked.

"Yes, it is my wish. I thought you said I was free to choose my suitor. Are you now trying to renege on your word?" she asked.

"Of course not, I just want to make sure you are serious about this." The father said.

"I am serious about it. I want only the most handsome man alive."

"Very well, it shall be as you wish," the chief said.

Thus, everyone that presented himself as a suitor, she turned away. She insisted that her devoted brother, Tomah, subject each to inspection.

Tomah was the completely opposite of his sister. He was as ugly as she was pretty. He was as kind as she was selfish. He was as considerate as she was thoughtless. He would change into an insect and enter the suitor's room when he slept. He would then inspect him carefully and if unsatisfied, he would report to his sister. This way he was able to tell each man's default. He loved his sister very much and did this to satisfy her wishes.

Tomah, was meticulous in his duty to his sister, he uncovered moles, spots, scars, warts ringworms, any many other defects some of which were battle wounds, or hunting wounds that these great men were proud of, but it turned out that, to this maiden, this did not matter.

One day, news reached Taywah that another handsome and wealthy suitor had come to ask her hand in marriage. This one was from a distant land that many had not heard about. In fact, no one present had visited this land, but it was rumored that it was richer and more prosperous than all the kingdoms in that part of the world. Taywah could not understand what all the fuss was about. Her maids were all urging here to not let this one slip her hand. They spoke of how handsome and well-built he was. As for the gifts he brought, they said that not all the gifts of every suitor before him could compare to his. They had taken all the chief's servants, and many more from subordinate kings to transport the gifts he brought along for her. Moreover, even with those many people, it still took them several trips to make the short journey.

When he concluded all the formalities, the Chief sent for Taywah. She came to the palace and to her surprise the suitor was all they said he was and more.

She did not expect such a perfection. She found herself secretly wishing he could pass the test, but again she was the most beautiful princess who was not going to settle for any less. If he did not pass, she would feel bad but she believed she deserved the best man in the whole world and nothing was going to stop her.

Thus, that night, Tomah set about his task. He changed into a fly to conduct his inspection. The fly buzzed around and around, searching the suitor's arms and legs, belly and chest and back for even the smallest blemish, but the skin of the suitor had none. In deep wonder, the ugly brother returned to his sister to report, "Oh sister," he announced, "this stranger's skin is perfect. There is no pimple, spot, or any mark. His skin is whole and pure, and beautiful to feel."

She said, "Seriously? Wow, that is amazing. Are you really sure Tomah?"

"Yes. I am sure of it. I checked many times over because I could not believe it myself," Tomah said.

"Then he is the first," and calmly added, "I shall marry him."

However, her brother was wise beyond his years, and devotion for her sharpened his natural wit. "Beloved sisters," he began, "be careful and please take time. There is something strange about this suitor I cannot yet define. He has an evil air. I feel he is too perfect and spotless for a human."

"Be quiet!" she yelled in her usual quick-tempered voice, "Who are you to judge a perfect man, or speak against him? A crooked, twisted, hunched backed creature such as you should learn to keep your place. And besides, I know that you are jealous of me and my good fortune." However, after she noticed her brother's sad continence, she changed her tone to a somewhat gentler one and asked, "Tomah, I am sorry. I didn't mean to hurt your feelings. It is just that I have been maiden too long. Don't you think?"

He nodded and said, "Yes, you have."

She continued, "Now you understand why I must take this suitor as quickly as possible?"

"I do." He again nodded, but he knew that she was only trying to make light of her earlier comments to him. Deep down he knew she meant everything she said.

Meanwhile, the suitor had entered the chief's court, splendidly dressed and presented all the fine presents to the chief. He had made his intentions to marry the chief's daughter known. He was proceeding along with the chief to continue the formalities. They were in the midst of this process and the chief thought, "What a nice looking man. Too sad he may be turned away like the others." He was partly sad but still hopeful. He listened to the suitor's request at length and offered him this advice. "Many great warriors, kings, nobles and princes have sat before me and made this very request, but each was turned down by my daughter. I hope you understand this and be prepared for whatever she decides."

"I understand chief," he said.

The chief continued, "Son, it seems to me you are a fine and worthy fellow, but my daughter might not take you. She seems to have in mind a particular kind of man that she wants to marry. If all was left with me, I would have married her out to one of the great suitors before you, or even you, but this is not my decision and whatever she decides I am honored bound to accept." He paused for a moment, and said, "I hope you succeed, I sincerely do." With that, he sent for Taywah and presented the suitor to her along with the gifts.

To his utmost surprise, after the presentation of the suitor, Taywah, showed a level of interest he had not seen in her before that moment. She lit up and glowed like a star. She actually blushed as she indicated to her father that she might just be interested in the suitor. Her father could not believe his eyes and thought he was dreaming. He needed to be sure, so he asked her, "What is your decision regarding the suitor?"

This time she told her father something else. "I know that my past actions worried you. I even know that you feared that if I kept it up, I might not get a decent husband, but I am prettiest maiden in the whole land and I deserve the very best,"

"Oh no, please no," her father thought. When he heard that, he sighed and shook his head repeatedly. This was her favorite line before she rejected a proposal. "What was I thinking?" he thought to himself. He knew he was mistaking her actions earlier.

Just when he could hide his disappointment no longer, Taywah said, "That is why I did not take those before. However father, I have decided not to let this suitor go away alone. I will accept his proposal."

"What!" the Chief said and jumped to his feet. He rushed to Taywah and hugged her. He abruptly let her go and shouted for the best town crier. He was taking no chances. He said, "Rush to the ends of the kingdom with as many assistants as you can manage. Keep announcing the greatest feast and wedding ceremony. You are to invite every subject in every village and make sure that all the nobles and great warriors are informed as well. They are requested to appear in court immediately." The mother of Taywah was happy beyond reckoning.

There was fanfare in the land. Many people seemed to have a positive opinion on the issue. Everyone seemed elated except Tomah whose views were the least sought. No one seemed to share his concern, or if anyone did, he or she did not dare voice it out.

Within hours of the proclamation of the Day of Days and the Week of Weeks, the city was dressed in gaiety and splendor for a festival surpassing any festival which ever went before. From towns and villages men came with gifts, hunters searched the forests for red meat, palms were tapped for wine, great cooking fires appeared and the best dancers and musicians of the land were summoned to perform.

Thus, it was that the lovely Taywah married the unknown suitor. She seemed happy as her ugly brother grieved alone, and some people wondered what it was which made him grieve.

The joyful chief gave the married couple one whole section across the river leading to the valley. They had cattle and goats, which needed at least shepherds to care adequately for them. He also gave them not just one but two whole towns of servants. He did all he could to persuade the suitor to live in his kingdom. He feared that the suitor would take his daughter far away and he would not be able to see her as often as he would like. Yet in a week and a day, the pair left on their journey to the stranger's distant land.

They travelled down to the coast following the St. Paul River and entered the suitor's long canoe, with gold, silver and some of the treasures the Chief had given them. As he paddled to sea with his bride, the suitor sang a song:

> *"Pa Ma Wei lei, ma ya pa;*
> *Pa Ma a lei!"*

The name of the suitor was Pa Ma, and the song he sang roughly translates:

> *"Pa Ma is going, going far away;*
> *Pa Ma sings farewell, forever!"*

Every time he came to the *wei* part, he paddled more aggressively, as fishermen do, so that the canoe sped swiftly and more swiftly out to sea.

When they were far at sea and winds began brushing water from the waves, he said the magic words and the ocean opened to them. Much to Taywah's surprise the canoe descended among frightful shadows and slimy things that crawled, clinched and slithered. The suitor shed the soft, smooth, spotless skin he had been wearing. Underneath the skin was a Ginah. He was hideous to look upon, a scaly thing with cruel eyes, Taywah shrank from him in fear and disgust and tried to run away, but with scabby claws he seized her, dragged her to the entrance of a silent cave, and into the dismal shadow- world beneath.

Nights passed and nothing improved. Night succeeded night, for under the sea, there are no days, just nights. There is not sufficient light. Taywah lived in natural fear of the Ginah and the shadowy shapes that watched her every move. Her one friend was the mother of the Ginah. She was compassionate and always encouraged Taywah to be strong.

One day she said to her, "Child, you are both beautiful and tenderhearted. What are you doing here? Why did you come? My son is cruel and wicked, much more than I care to admit. Many are the girls he has lured here from the land and he has destroyed and devoured then all. Surely, this will be your fate. I fear for you!"

From then onwards, the poor bride lived in hourly fear of death. She wept, she sobbed, she prayed and she would not eat. Still nothing changed for her. Then, after days of sobbing, weeping, praying and not eating, a fly buzzed gently by her face.

"A fly?" she thought, "but there were no flies under the sea." She ceased her weeping and looked up to find her ugly little brother standing by her side. Her eyes grew wide in wonder and delight, "Oh, beloved brother! Oh, how did you get here?"

"Hush, let us waste no time," her brother urged her. "I travelled with you in the canoe, for I feared something evil might happen to you, but when we got here, the Ginah hid the box I was hiding in under a table. I escaped today when one of his prisoners went to clean up."

She was so relieved to see him that she reached out grab him but he flew away. He was still a fly and if she crushed him, it would be over. "Oh, sorry," she said as she burst out laughing for the first time in a long time. So, how do we get out of here?"

"I think I might know a way. I have discovered the Ginah's magic box. We need to sneak out through the secret doorway he uses and get to the other end of the cave. The canoe is waiting. It is time to go!"

Hand in hand, they ran through dark tunnels curtained with waiving seaweed, through rocky places where sea-animals on thin logs clicked and scuttled, and past the gaping mouths of caves, and came to the canoe. Her brother had stolen the Ginah's box of magic secrets. When they reached near the river, he stopped to say the magic words he'd heard the Ginah mutter, as Taywah opened the box just after he finished.

Boom! Out flew a more fearsome Ginah. It rushed to attack them, then suddenly stopped. It spoke in a terrifying voice, "Who are you people? What are you doing here?"

They told their story. Then the Ginah said, "I have been held captive in that box for fifty years by the sea Ginah but now I am free, thanks to you. Since you saved me I will grant you one request."

"We wish to go home." They said.

"Very well then," said the Ginah. "You will get your wish, however, before I do so, you must know something about the magic box. At all times one person must be in the box for its magic to work. It takes two persons to open the box, one says the words, the other opens the box. That is the rule of the box and there is no other way around it."

The question is, who will go into the box and who will go home? One person spoke the words, the other opened the box, so both were responsible for freeing the Ginah yet, only one will live freely on land. Who will that be?

ABOUT THE AUTHOR

The author is an educator, folklorist, writer and social commentator. He has written extensively on Liberia and other social issues. His work experiences and years of travel have added an extra dimension to his works. He is passionate for his native land and preserving its history, cultures, and traditions.

His education covers several disciplines and he actively promotes the New Liberia concept of a mental revolution. He is the founder of the Liberia GiveBack Project and he heads the newly establish Liberian think tank Everything Liberia (http://othnieldf.wix.com/everythingliberia)

He currently resides in Asia with his family where he works as an educator and continues to dedicate his time to writing.